D0425422

Carnegie Public Library
202 N. Animas St.
Trinidad, CO 81082-2643

THE COLOR OF FIRE

THE
COLOR
OF
FIRE

A NOVEL

Ann Rinaldi

JUMP AT THE SUN

HYPERION BOOKS FOR CHILDREN

NEW YORK

Carnegie Public Library
202 N. Animas St.
Trinidad, CO 81082-2643

Text copyright © 2005 by Ann Rinaldi

All rights reserved.

No part of this book may be reproduced or transmitted in any form or by
any means, electronic or mechanical, including photocopying, recording, or by
any information storage and retrieval system, without written permission
from the publisher. For information address
Hyperion Books for Children,

114 Fifth Avenue, New York, New York 10011-5690.

Printed in the United States of America

First Edition

1 3 5 7 9 10 8 6 4 2

Reinforced binding

Library of Congress Cataloging-in-Publication Data on file.

ISBN 0-7868-0938-8

5-20-05

Visit www.jumpatthesun.com

In memory of my uncle Anthony

THE COLOR OF FIRE

CHAPTER ONE

*I*T A L L started with Jacobus Stroutenburgh's breeches.

He was on the roof next to my master's house that day in April when my master's warehouse caught fire. What he was doing on the roof next door is anybody's guess. He always was a queer one, that Jacobus Stroutenburgh. How many times did he complain about me to my mistress! I'd stepped on his tulip bed. I'd let my master's dog relieve himself on his lawn.

Likely he was enjoying the sight of my master's storehouse burning on the waterfront, watching the red and yellow flames eat up the shingles, watching the black smoke, the people below running around and screaming. He was there when he saw a Negro sneak out the window of a nearby storehouse and begin to run.

To give credit where credit is due, Jacobus started to work his way down the roof to catch the Negro, who he suspected had set the fires. But his breeches got caught on a nail. And being the skinflint he was, old Jacobus didn't want to tear them, so instead he started yelling, "A Negro running, a Negro running!"

This is about the worst thing a person can say in New York. Almost as bad as yelling "Fire! Fire!" because both are calculated to arouse the people and provoke their innermost fears.

The mob below heard Jacob and picked up his panic, as if it were a ball thrown to them.

And the mob grabbed the ball and made it into the shape they wanted. They started to yell, "The Negroes are rising! The Negroes are rising!"

I was in the yard feeding the chickens when Cuffee lumbered through the gate. And lumbered is the only way to describe the way he ran.

Because he was big and round. And every bit as good-natured as his size.

"Where are you going?" I called out.

"I gotta hide. They're after me."

"Why?"

"Because." And he stood there, breathless, but still his arrogant self. "Because, Phoebe, I'm the Negro who is rising up."

Then he ran into the house through the back door.

I laughed. Only because I didn't think Cuffee, with his silk breeches and the rest of his fine feathers, knew what it meant to rise up. We all understood that and we all loved him anyway. He couldn't rise up if the Lord himself asked him to.

The mob, which was by then ten or twelve people strong, ran to our front door. To the front door of my master Adolph Philipse's grand house, and he one of the most powerful men in town because he was the speaker of the New York Assembly. They pounded on the door. Agnes, the white indentured servant, answered and they surged in, without so much as a by-your-leave, past my mistress, who was in her chair, enjoying being downstairs for a day, and was ready to faint dead away. They ran through the house and into the back, where the kitchen was. Where Cuffee was. The next thing I saw was them dragging Cuffee out.

"To jail!" they shouted. "To jail!"

Mr. Ury, who taught me my lessons, said that was the peculiar thing about a mob. It had so many legs and arms, but only one head. Like a caterpillar.

I stood by the side gate and watched them go. *Cuffee will be all right*, I told myself. *He always is all right. His sass will get him out of this just like it gets him out of every trouble he ever got into.*

But inside me something said, *No, this is different.* It was bad that Cuffee started to run. He never should have run.

I heard my mistress weeping just inside the door, heard Agnes trying to quiet her. Heard the chickens clucking at my feet and the crackling of flames from our burning storehouse, which was only a little bit away. But because it was near City Hall, on Broad and Wall streets, the town's fire engines were on the scene right off. My master never liked those fire engines. Always said there was nothing wrong with the old bucket brigade. He'd been on many a bucket brigade in his time, too, and now there were the newfangled fire engines pumping water right out of the river.

Our house was on a little rise, so you could stand on the walk out front and see all three of my master's storehouses. The middle one was burning but, thanks to the help of so many people, the fire was soon put out.

The wind, always off the water, blew ashes and soot our way and soon my eyes were stinging me. I emptied out the chicken feed bucket and put it back by the barn door and walked into the house.

It was pretty much a shambles. Tables and chairs were overturned. The curtains were pulled from the windows, the Persian carpets trampled with mud. How could they have done so much harm in so little time?

"Phoebe, go and get the master," Agnes ordered.

She was standing over Mistress, who was weeping. "I want my husband. Agnes, get me my husband."

"I've sent for him, ma'am." Agnes was nothing if not in charge at all times.

"Go, Phoebe," she scolded. "At once."

I went outside and started in the direction of City Hall. People were gathered on the walks, pointing to the warehouse, and I heard snatches of conversation as I walked along.

I heard "Fire purposely laid," and "Just like Mrs. Hilton's house last Saturday night," and "It's the Negroes. They ought to take them up."

The phrases whirled around in my head and connected into a chant. Then someone saw me. "Isn't that Mrs. Philipse's Negro girl there? Look at her, walking around like she can go where she pleases. They ought to put a stop to that."

I hurried on. The sun was warm, but there were still patches of slush lying about from the terrible winter. Yet in some places I saw yellow flowers peeking through the wet grasses. *Why don't they just look at the flowers?* I asked myself. They haven't even seen the flowers. And after the terrible winter we had, you'd think flowers would be pleasing to them now. Wouldn't you think? Especially yellow ones. Yellow, Mr. Ury always told us, is the color of hope.

CHAPTER TWO

*A*T CITY HALL they said they'd last seen my master at the wharf, across the street, so I went there, where the crowd was gathered. I asked if they'd seen Cuffee. They said a mob had come in with a Negro, but it wasn't our Cuffee. I breathed a sigh of relief. Knowing Cuffee, he'd already outwitted them.

"Here it is, eighteen days after Fort George was left in ashes," I heard someone say, "and now another fire. What are we to think?"

I recognized the voice as belonging to Abigail Earle.

"I don't know," said her companion, Lydia George. "But I see someone who might. Isn't that Assemblyman Philipse's little housemaid? What's her name again?"

I felt eyes on me. "Phoebe," said Abigail. "Cuffee lives with them."

"Ho there, Phoebe!" Abigail called out to me. They were meddling fishwives, but if I didn't obey and pay respect they'd be on at my master about me. So I walked over.

"Yes, ma'am?"

"What do you know about the fire?"

Such a stupid question. What could I know? I saw a few heads turn to stare at me and got frightened for a moment. "No more than anybody else," I said.

"What does your master think?"

"I haven't seen him since this one started. I've been sent to fetch him home. My mistress has need of him."

"Well, I'll tell you what I know." Abigail lowered her voice. "All the King's men, those who run things in this city, believe it to be the work of the Negroes. That's what I heard already this morning."

A quick intake of breath from her friend. *That be all we need*, I thought. Gossip like that. And I moved away, excusing myself.

I circled the edge of the crowd, hearing snatches of conversation along the way.

"It isn't enough that we have hostilities with Spain," I heard one man say, "and that this past winter had so near buried us alive that people were having a bad time with money. Now, fire."

"Well, I saw three black men walking along and they were talking about fire early this morning, and one of them was Quacko."

Everybody in town knew everybody else's Negroes and who they traveled about with. And everybody knew that our Cuffee hung about with Quacko.

Oh, I was afraid. To good-natured Cuffee it would all be a prank. If he was involved in an uprising, all it meant was that they were using him.

Then I caught sight of my master, almost the same time as he saw me. I was so glad of his familiar stance that I ran to him. "Master."

"Phoebe. What are you doing here? Are things all right at home?"

"Yes, sir, but Mistress is crying. Agnes sent me for you."

He nodded. He tucked his hat under his left arm. He ran his hand through his hair. He looked about. His black coat was covered with ashes and his face was turning the same grayish color. "Where's Cuffee?" he asked me.

"I don't know. A crowd came by the house and took him away, but I think he escaped."

"Well, you find him for me, will you, Phoebe? Bring him home. I've got to get on there myself. Nothing more can be done here. The fire's almost out."

"Yes, sir."

He put a hand on my shoulder and patted it. He was nothing if not kind. I watched him go and turned to scan the crowd.

Cuffee would stand out if he were here. He wasn't. So I turned in the only direction I could to find out his whereabouts. I turned in the direction of Hughson's tavern.

I could see Mary Burton at least, and she could tell me what was going on. Mary always knew the latest gossip.

The loud talk died down as I opened the door and entered. I couldn't see at first, coming in from the brightness outside to the dimness inside. But I felt everyone looking at me and was glad I'd put my shawl half over my face. For only an instant they stared, though, and then they went back to their business. Seeing Assemblyman Philipse's little slave girl Phoebe in here wasn't anything new, after all. I came all the time to get his dram and fetch it home.

They went back to their card playing, their dice throwing, their talk about cockfights and what ships had docked late yesterday and what ship's master had come in looking for men to sign on with his crew.

Had they been talking of the fires? Most likely. But they were all hulking shadows to me, bent over the tables—the ne'er-do-wells, the sailors off the ships—all but the Hughsons, who owned the place; their daughter, Sarah; the servant girl Peggy; and their sixteen-year-old indentured servant girl, Mary Burton.

I went to the bar. "Hello, Phoebe. What can I do for you?" Mrs. Hughson asked.

"I'm looking for Cuffee."

She laughed. "So is everybody else in town."

"Was he in here?"

"He was just in here and left. Someone

came and told him he'd best do that. He's gone, child. Escaped from the mob somehow." She seemed about to impart some other information to me, when out of the corner came Mary Burton.

"Hello, Phoebe."

"Hello, Mary."

"Did you hear about the fire?"

"I did."

She pushed me with her hip, a habit she had. At the same time she winked. It all meant mischief was afoot. Mary always knew about the mischief that was afoot.

"Guess what, Phoebe?"

"What?"

"I'm going to be free one of these days. No more indenture."

Such talk put me on notice. An indentured servant suddenly becoming free did not necessarily mean good things. "How?"

"I listen. And I learn," she whispered so Mrs. Hughson couldn't hear. "And when the time comes, I can tell."

"Tell what?"

"Whatever needs to be told." She loved talking in riddles. It made her sound as if she knew things the rest of us didn't.

Out of a back room then came Elizabeth Luckstead, Mrs. Hughson's mother.

I knew her to tell fortunes. Everyone did. Some people said she was a witch. Others simply put her down as crazy. She looked the part of either; with her mobcap half off her head, her hair disheveled, and her long fingers with nails the color of indigo.

"Hello, Mrs. Luckstead," I said.

"Phoebe Philipse, come join our circle. Come, people!" she called out to everyone. "I'm going to do a spell."

"Not now, Mama. This isn't the time for spells," Mrs. Hughson called out to her, but she paid no nevermind. Just went to the middle of the wooden floor.

"Mary, get me my magic stick." Mary knew just what to do, of course. She went to the hearth where a fire burned and picked up a piece of wood that was charred on the bottom and gave it to Mrs. Luckstead, who made a curtsy then as if she were wearing salmon-colored silk.

I know what I saw. And I will remember it always. Though I should have gotten out, then and there, I didn't. I stayed, and I saw her make a black ring on the old wooden floor with the piece of half-burned wood. I saw her make all the Negroes present put their left foot in the ring. Then they all turned to me, waiting.

"Come on, Phoebe," Mary said. "Take the oath."

"What oath?"

"The sacred oath." She reached out and grabbed my hand and pulled me toward the circle. Obediently I put my left foot in. Then Mrs. Luckstead said some kind of mumbly words and held a bowl of punch over our heads. Then she said, so all could understand: "Thunder and lightning, God's curse and hellfire, fall on them that first discover the plot."

That's what she said. The plot.

And every Negro present repeated the words after her. Including me. Then she gave them a draught from the punch bowl. But I got out of the circle before it came round to me. And then she herself drank.

I shivered, watching it. I turned away. And in turning I saw Mr. Ury, my teacher. He was seated at the end of the bar, drinking: not at all like the Mr. Ury I knew who taught me my sums and my words.

He looked at me. He raised his glass. And, not wanting to acknowledge him, I turned from him and looked back to the witch's circle. It went easier on my eyes than seeing my dear Mr. Ury sitting there drinking and saying nothing to all the nonsense going on about him.

I know what I saw. I know what I took part in. And I shall not forget it.

CHAPTER THREE

I CAST A WORRIED eye around me all the way home, but I ran into no trouble. The streets were now quiet and the smell of smoke was all around. It drifted in the air, coming from the smoldering ruins of the warehouse.

I wondered if my master would speak up for Cuffee. He'd often done so, always with the warning that he'd never do it again. But always he did it again.

As for me, Cuffee had just always been there for me.

I'd been with the Philipses since I was ten. Before that is like a blur, though I have memories of my mother bending over me, feeding me, and even punishing me when I did wrong. I just cannot separate any of it into days or years. I don't know where my father was, but my mother was a servant to the Van Cortlands. They were people of ruffles, as we Negroes like to say. People who had money and ran things in town. Their house had high ceilings and tall windows and rich woodwork and carpets.

But then things to do with money got bad for Mr. Van Cortland and then, too, my mother died. I was not old enough to take her place as Mrs. Van Cortland's personal servant, so I was sent to the almshouse.

Slaves who are children are not worth much. It takes too long to feed them and train them up to do a good job. The most valuable are the men like Cuffee. And Mr. Roosevelt's Quacko and Mr. Todd's Dundee. There are a score of them here in New York, all body servants or coachmen to the King's men. Cuffee runs with them. They all have fancy clothes and more money than poor white folk. They earn it from tips and visitors at their masters' fancy houses. Many white folk have bad things to say about them.

They are all spoiled. They all know how important they are.

Last winter, for instance, when the big snow came so high that you couldn't walk in it, and the weather so cold that the squirrels froze in the streets and the Hudson River was a sheet of ice, so cold that the poor died in their homes, Cuffee knew where to get a cord of wood for less than forty shillings, the going price. Men like Mr. Philipse depend on their body servants for things like that, besides knowing how hot they like their water for shaving and just how much starch they want in the ruffles of their shirts.

Anyway, when I was at the almshouse, and not yet ten, Mr. Ury came to visit. It wasn't a bad place, I suppose, a two-story stone-and-brick building on the Common at the northern out-skirts of town. There I was, with my mother dead and not a soul to call my own, wondering whether I was a "poor needy person," an "idle wandering vagabond," or a "sturdy beggar," as the sign said out front.

It was part of Mr. Ury's ministry to visit

these and other "petty rogues and criminals," though he claimed not to be a minister. He was a teacher who called his work his ministry. And part of that ministry was coming to visit the children in the almshouse. He started to teach me history and geography in that almshouse. I had never been taught such before.

I knew from the onset that there was something different about Mr. Ury, or at least something people perceived to be different. For one thing, he was just there in town one day, without so much as a by-your-leave, with none of the letters of introduction that white folk so prize, and nobody to vouch for him. He came off almost as a Negro without papers. This alone made people suspicious of him.

New York City was, after all, just a small town. Everyone knew everyone. Mr. Ury, furthermore, did not present himself in a social manner, did not advertise himself as a teacher. He just started teaching.

Just as he came to the almshouse and started to teach me to read. And just about the time I learned (and I shall never forget the joy in learning) he came one day to take me home, he said.

"Home?" I asked. "But I don't have a home. I have no place, no people."

"You do now," he told me. "Assemblyman Philipse has need of a little girl about the house just like you. His wife, Annette, is bound to a chair from what she calls 'the spreading sickness.'"

"What is that?" I asked.

"Her joints swell and hurt. It isn't catching. Some people call it arthritis. And that dear lady is in much pain."

So I went with Mr. Ury. And, whether at his request or not I do not know, but they allowed him to keep coming to the house to teach me.

I do know that Mistress wanted me to read to her. It was why I was taught to read. And so I did. And Mr. Ury, who knew about the world outside New York, spoke of it to me.

He also spoke about God as if he conferred with Him every day. He was kind and gentle and I grew to love him.

I'm fourteen now, but I know my sums, my reading, my Bible.

I've known Cuffee for four years. He was at the Philipses' when I got there. His aged mother works there, too. His father used to, before he was killed in a riot, years ago. I don't think

Cuffee knows the whole cloth of it. His mother mentions it on occasion, when she warns Cuffee not to turn out like his father, and she and Mistress Annette exchange glances. But no one speaks of it.

Some people say Cuffee is not quite right in the head. It isn't that. He's as sane as a preacher's wife. He's just fun loving, is all. Doesn't worry about a thing. He loves to dress up in the fine clothes the master gives him, loves to wear a wig and serve dinner in style. Loves it when company comes and he can show off his manners. I've seen him and his friend Prince with money in their hands. Spanish doubloons. Cuffee is always out for a good time.

One word from Master and he quiets right down, though. That's all it takes. One word. It doesn't take a mob to do it.

Sometimes, alone with me, he jokes about running away. "Where would you go?" I ask.

"To the Senecas," he says, "the Onondagas, the other Indian tribes to the north. They would give me refuge. They have given it to others. Or mayhap to the Montauks, the Shinnecocks, the Massapequas on eastern Long Island."

The names of the Indian tribes drip off his

tongue like honey, as if he is well acquainted with them. And I feel such envy. But then I know he doesn't really mean it. He's treated too well around here. But he is saying what I some-

e long days when Mistress
ring is in the air and my
I want to go somewhere
off and be free. Run to
lagas and be taken in as
I am sure they would
ms, as they have wel-
o Cuffee told me.

ke you a slave," he
way."

now."

w to get there," he
minds me that he
I know Doctor
icine home from

a Negro doctor
s of the city to
knew he was more witch doctor than medicine doctor, but everybody liked him. Everybody except the King's men. Anyway, Cuffee did know how to get to

CHAPTER FOUR

"PSST! PHOEBE. Over here."

I knew whose voice it was, recognized it in an instant. I was just about to mount the back steps of the house when I heard it from the direction of the stables.

"Cuffee?"

"Hush. You gotta hush or I'm a dead man."

I ran toward the voice. He was just inside the stable door. "What are you doing out here?"

"Feedin' the horses. You think they don't

wanna eat? You think they care that I'm a no-good troublemaker? Don't matter to them, the food tastes the same."

"No, I mean aren't you under arrest?"

"I am. But I got away."

I felt a pang of panic. "And you came here?"

"Sure. It's the last place a mob will look fer me. Only I don't want my mama to see me neither. She'll beat me with a broom, fer sure."

"Oh, Cuffee." I hugged him around his ample waist. "What can I do for you?"

"Stop that fool cryin', fer one thing. Who needs your tears? Listen, Phoebe, I need you to go in the house and get my coat and hat and grab somethin' fer me to eat, without bein' seen."

"That's like asking a cat not to sneak up on a mouse. Why do you need these things? Where are you going?"

"You need to ask? I'm leavin', Phoebe. Goin' to Long Island an' the Indians. I got friends there."

"You can't go," I said. I didn't know how I'd keep him, but I knew I would. I couldn't let him leave. "Without you the household will be nothing."

"I'm goin' somewhere. If not to Indians, to jail."

"No, Master will speak for you. Why, Mistress can't even get up the stairs without you carrying her. Master would be lost without you. You know that."

"But I disappointed them both, Phoebe. An' you know what that does to me."

"Then why were you involved with the fires?"

"I wasn't. I was just around the warehouse. I started running when they yelled that a Negro was running. 'Cause I got scared. An' after that everybody wants to hang me."

I stamped my foot. "Nobody is going to hang you, Cuffee. Not while I have breath left in me."

"Oh yeah? What you gonna do, Phoebe. Forbid them?"

"No. I'm going in the house right now and telling Master you're out here and you're innocent. And that you want to come inside but are fearful. You know how fond he is of you. Now let me go and I'll do it."

But he hung on to my arm. "You're too trustin', Phoebe. What if he ain't fond of me no more?"

"He is," I said. "You know Master isn't the kind to let people push him around."

"Ain't you afeared of his anger?"

"Yes, but you'd do it for me, wouldn't you?"

He didn't say anything. He didn't have to.

Agnes started in on me the minute I walked in the back door. "Mistress wants you. Where you been? Seems like alla time I'm makin' excuses for either you or Cuffee."

"Did the master come home?"

"Oh, he's home, all right. Waitin' for the first one who comes through that door."

"Does he know about Cuffee?"

"He knows there's a price on his head. What else is there to know? He just got back from the magistrate's office where he went to get him free. Only Cuffee ain't there."

"Where is Mistress?"

"In the dinin' room, waitin'. Where else can she go without Cuffee to lift her chair?"

Yes, I thought. *They need Cuffee around here.* And I knew what I would do then. I would put it in front of their eyes how they needed him. And I would make Mistress help me. I felt no shame whatsoever as I walked into the center hall and curtsied to her.

"I'm sorry I'm late, Mistress," I said.

She was in her chair with the wheels. Master

had had it made for her. Now they couldn't get it upstairs.

"Phoebe, where have you been? Don't I have enough on my mind this day without worrying about you?"

"I was out. First looking for Master, then Cuffee."

"On the streets? With a mob loose? I forbid you to go on the streets again until all this nonsense is settled. Do you hear?"

"Yes, Mistress."

Agnes brought in a tray with a bowl of soup. I fetched the bowl and spooned some into her mouth, then wiped her mouth with a snow-white napkin. She was prone to nerves. I saw her hands trembling.

"Tell my husband I want him out here," she said.

"Mayhap you can help me, ma'am," I ventured. "I have to talk with him. Only I'm afeared. Would you come to his study with me?"

"Posh," she waved away a hand. "He's the kindest man I've ever known. Now, I won't have you being afraid of him. What have you to tell him? Do you know where Cuffee is?"

My heart was beating very fast. "Yes, ma'am."

"Well then, let's go." And she slammed down her polished cane on the floor. "Lead away, child."

"Master?"

He was behind his desk, ruffling through newspapers.

"Mr. Philipse," she said to him.

He looked up. "Ah, yes, Mrs. Philipse. How are you bearing up? No more mobs at the front door, I presume."

"I would have you pay mind to this child. She knows where Cuffee is."

His eyes narrowed. He put down his pen. He scowled and I trembled. "Phoebe, is this true?"

"Yes, sir."

"Well? Tell me."

I wanted to talk to him first, to make him promise he would see that no harm came to Cuffee before I told. But I could not, for the life of me, bring myself to do that.

"Please don't punish him. He's been running all this time and hiding. And he's afeared you'll put him out or have the King's men come for him. Please, Mr. Philipse, Cuffee had naught to do with the fires."

"Come here, Phoebe," was all he said.

So I went to him. I let him take my hand and pull me close. "Did you ever hear of the Negro revolt of 1712, child?"

"I heard mention of it."

"Mention! Well, it deserves more than that. What has Mr. Ury been teaching you? In 1712, twenty-three Negroes gathered in the middle of the night of April sixth, armed with hatchets, knives, swords, and guns they'd stolen from their masters. They set fire to some buildings here in New York and when the people came out to put out the fires, they set upon them. They shot, beat, and stabbed nine whites to death, and wounded six before they were taken in hand. The town fathers had to call in the militia from as far as Westchester. They captured them all. They executed some by hanging, some by burning them alive. Six committed suicide."

"Cuffee's father was one of them," Mistress added.

My heart flipped. "Does Cuffee know?"

"Of course he knows," she went on. "His father was burned alive."

I could not speak. I could not get the words

past my ears and into my head. "What of Cuffee's mother?" I asked. "What of Old Rose?"

"Old Rose held Cuffee and watched. He was a babe in her arms. And that is why she is so strict with him, so hard. He has the same nature as his father," Mistress said.

"Now," Master put in, "if you want to save your friend from the same fate, show me where he is hiding. I'll have to go down to the magistrate's office this very hour and explain things away."

CHAPTER FIVE

*M*Y MASTER didn't scold Cuffee. He didn't even question him. He just took him off to the magistrate's office and Cuffee went away meekly, trusting Mr. Philipse to do the proper thing by him. I stayed close the rest of that day, waiting for them to come home. They came around supper time.

At last, Cuffee was home. He was in the house. He served at the table, something my master liked him to do. The food tasted better when Cuffee served it, he always said.

I didn't realize until I undressed for bed that night how much my skirt and chemise and apron smelled of smoke. And that night there was another fire. Captain Peter Warren's house, and he a brother-in-law of Chief Justice DeLancey. Master would allow neither Cuffee nor me out that night. After supper, long after sunset, Mary Burton came to our back door.

"They've jailed my master and mistress," she said.

"Who has jailed them?"

"The town magistrates. They feel they must do something."

She stood there at our kitchen door, holding her basket. I invited her in.

Since the fire of last night, nothing seemed normal anymore. The King's men were jailing everybody. The King's men promised money to those who would talk. They wanted to loosen tongues.

Governor George Clarke, Esquire, had turned out the garrison and ordered the troops to stand night watch until further notice. He knew the city was a tinderbox of hate and blame and suspicion.

The town fathers knew they had to do something. So they arrested people.

I was just preparing a tray of after-dinner tea for my mistress. "Wait until I take this upstairs," I told Mary.

Then Cuffee stepped forward. "I'll take it up, Phoebe." And he took the tray from my hands.

"So he's out of jail," Mary said.

"Yes. He never was in jail," I told her. "But my master made a lot of high talk to make sure of that."

"Isn't your master taking a chance by doing such?"

"He's loyal to Cuffee. But he called us all together the other night and said he would do it once. Just once would he speak up for any of us if we're jailed. Cuffee knows that after this, he's on his own."

"Well, he should stay out of our tavern then. Tell him that. It's where they all gather."

"Who?"

"Come on, Phoebe, you know. The trouble-makers."

"Cuffee isn't one of them."

"He certainly doesn't look the part of a rogue now, I must say. Though I've seen him playing the part in our tavern. By the way, I stopped by to tell you, the tavern will remain open. I'll be running it."

"You?" I near scoffed.

"Yes. I can do it as well as my master and mistress. Talk is," she said as she took the cup of tea I handed her, "talk is, the people are looking for someone to blame for the fires. A white person. A mastermind of the plan."

"They've got your master and mistress."

"No. They couldn't mastermind anything. They're looking for a white male." And she gazed at me significantly, as if I should know one.

"Now I've been called before the grand jury tomorrow morning," she went on. "And I'm going to give King's evidence. I'm going to talk and be set free, Phoebe. I've made my mind up."

I stared at her. "You? Free? How?"

"They're giving money and freedom to any indentured servant or slave who will talk. I can get a hundred pounds and my freedom if I tell what I know. You can get twenty. And be set free."

"But neither of us knows anything."

Now she did scoff. "I know what I know, Phoebe. And you do too. It was in the paper this day. You could be free this spring."

I thought of the Indian tribes with the names that dripped like honey. I thought of what Long Island must look like in spring. "You could talk too," she whispered. "Tell what you know."

"I know nothing."

She smiled. "A schoolteacher named Elias Neau was implicated in the plots of 1712," she said.

I felt a shiver of fear.

"Don't think people don't have their eyes on your Mr. Ury."

"Why?"

"I told you about the schoolteacher in the slave uprising last time. People are asking, how does Mr. Ury worship God? He's joined none of the city's congregations. He's not presented himself socially to the best families. And he can forgive sins."

"What?"

"It's eerie. He says he can forgive sins. I have suspicions about him, Phoebe. And you know that John Hughson's wife was brought up to be a Papist. And so was Peggy, who works for them. And Mr. Ury knows Latin. How does he know that language? It's the language of the papists. All that mumbling so nobody can understand.

There is a Catholic conspiracy afoot to subvert the crown. Everybody knows it. Everybody sees Ury as an agent of Spain."

"He isn't. He's a dear learned man."

"I'm going to get called to give King's evidence in court. They are going to want to know if Ury has been a frequent visitor at Hughson's. I'm going to say yes, he has."

"So have a lot of other men."

"But they don't speak Latin or go about saying they will forgive your sins. You know, Phoebe, I haven't taken the oath. They offered me silks and fine things if I would, my master and mistress. But I have said no."

"Yet you made me take it."

"I wanted to see if you would. You didn't, really. You had to be forced into the ring. That doesn't count."

And then she told me what did count. The Marshalls, the Moores, the Pintards were missing silk fabric, crystal, sterling from their houses. In their search of suspicious places the constables had found these things at Hughson's bar. "They've been fencing stolen goods for such a long time now," she told me. "And I suspected it."

She told me that Councilman Horsmanden,

who was running the investigation, sat heavy on crime. "He's a true King's man," she said. "His father was a pastor in England."

And she told me this: "You know how Cuffee and Prince run together all the time?"

"Yes."

"Well, Prince is angry. He's angry at the governor because that man won't let Prince visit his wife, who is the governor's cook. You ought to tell Cuffee to stay away from Prince. Or he'll soon be arrested again," she said.

When she left, my spirit was cast down and my mind was spinning. I saw myself falling into that circle Mrs. Luckstead had drawn on the tavern floor, unable to get out of it.

CHAPTER SIX

I MIGHT BE ONLY fourteen, but I knew I was sitting in the heart of something and that heart was beating rapidly right now.

Here I was, working in the house of a powerful man. I didn't know what my master did when he went to the assembly, but I knew he had power. Look how one word from him had gotten Cuffee out of trouble.

Here I was, asked if Cuffee runs with Prince.

Here I was, a frequent customer at Hughson's,

where I went for my master's daily dram. I have seen the gatherings there, heard the many Negroes talking.

Here I was, knowing it is a violation of the law for three or more Negroes to gather any-where and talk.

And here I was, a friend of Mary Burton's, she who says she is going to talk and tell things and gain her freedom. What things will she tell? And about whom?

And last, here I was, a friend of Mr. Ury's, and they are casting suspicious eyes upon him.

Mary said I must talk too, if they summon me. What do I have to say? I have seen things, may-hap the same things Mary has seen in Hughson's bar. I have seen more than three Negroes huddled together talking. I have heard hard words against masters. I have heard bitterness after the terrible winter we had, when so many of the poor died.

I have heard the words of envy against the Cuffees in town.

Any of this, or all of it, might serve to feed the fires of discontent that burn amidst us now. Any or all of it might put more people in jail. So all I can do is keep my head down and my mouth shut, and one thought in my mind.

Carnegie Public Library
202 N. Animas St.
Trinidad, CO 81082-2643

That even if I knew something important, I would not send a friend to jail to gain my own freedom. That is as far as I have gone in figuring out what I am going to do. And what I am not going to do. The idea that I could tell things to the King's men to get my own freedom never leaves me, of course. Not since Mary gave it to me.

After all, I am not a saint. The idea of my own freedom tantalizes me. It hangs in front of me like a yellow light in a black cave. It lurks in the shadows of the room like a white ghost. I do not know what I would do with it if I had it, of course. Because I can't get around the simple idea of just having it.

I think about it more and more each day.

But I must think of other things. I must speak with both Mr. Ury and Cuffee and try to decide where they stand in the pattern of things. And where they want to stand.

After all, things have changed for all of us now. The fires in town have burned new lines, separating some of us and bringing others closer together. I just needed to know how close, or far apart, those fires had made Cuffee and Mr. Ury is all.

* * *

Two days later there were more fires. First came Van Zant's warehouse on the docks by the East River. A bucket brigade helped this time. But the warehouse went up like a child's toy, with its dry, rotted wood frame bursting into colors and sparks of blue and orange.

The other was the fire that raged through Quick and Vergereau's cow stable at the foot of Maiden Lane. It was filled with dry fodder. The cows were crying and a passerby answered their call for help. Those flames were orange and red.

"Phoebe, I wish you to go to the end of town, by the pond. They say Doctor Harry is coming today," my master told me.

"Yes, sir."

My master took some shillings out of his pocket and gave them to me. "I wish you to buy some medicine. My wife is in great pain."

"Yes, Master." I often did this when Doctor Harry came to town. He came from Nassau, way out on that long island. Word travels quickly when he comes, as quickly as it can in the slave underground. And I figured that Cuffee must have told my master that Doctor Harry was coming. It was only one of the dozens of little personal favors he performed for Mr. Philipse that the good man could not do without.

Cuffee liked our master. And so did I. I know most slaves complain, but we have little to complain about, except that we are not free. But our lives could change if Master dies. Cuffee has reminded me of that. We could be sold to someone cruel and mean. And we must think of that. Master is an upstanding man. A powerful man. A man of good parts. But he is not God.

Doctor Harry is Negro, but he is not a slave. A lot of white folk in town depend on him for medicines. But he is not allowed in town. So he sets himself up by the pond which is just beyond the outskirts.

He comes with his simples, his remedies for sickness. The town magistrates have long since threatened him with whipping if he comes inside the city limits. They have accused him of not practicing medicine properly. But when I go there to buy for my mistress, I see the slaves from many a town magistrate's kitchen there to buy in secret.

Doctor Harry's remedies oftimes work better than those of the town doctors.

"Be careful," Master admonished as I took up my basket and left the house. "Speak as little as possible to anyone."

"May the first thunder strike me dead if I do, Master."

"Don't talk like that, Phoebe. It's slave talk. We have educated you to speak better."

"Yes, sir."

I took up my basket. If questioned I could always say I was on my way to the Old Slip Market on Burger's Path. Or the Fly Market on Maiden Lane. The day was fine and I wasn't above a nice walk. And I hadn't seen Doctor Harry in a while. He always told me about the Indians on "the island that was long." He moved amidst them, and I think that's where he got his remedies.

The pond was still and calm when I got there, with scarce a ripple on its surface. Scores of daffodils grew around it and the blue sky mirrored itself in it. I saw Doctor Harry right off, halfway around the sandy shore. His voice carried over the water as did those of the two slaves I saw with him.

I recognized them at once: Mr. Marshall's York and Mr. Costa's Sunday. I waited until they finished their business with Doctor Harry and walked into the woods, and then I approached him.

"Ah, the little Philipse girl." He was a short man, well-spoken and sincere. "How may I help you today?"

"I need some of the regular simples for my mistress. We have no more left, and she is in pain."

"How is that grand lady?"

"As I said, in pain when she doesn't have your simples. My master said to give as much as you can spare. I have money."

I lifted the napkin in my basket and he put the medicines, which were wrapped in large leaves, in it. I covered it again with the napkin. "Be careful. It is valuable," he urged me.

"I know."

He gave me a sly smile. "Any more fires in town?"

He knew everything. Nobody can figure out how, but he is no stranger to the doings in New York. "Not yet," I said.

"I hear your master came to Cuffee's aid."

"Yes. He told the magistrates never did he have such a faithful servant."

"From what I have heard about Assembly-man Philipse, next time he won't, you know."

I said nothing.

"Tell Cuffee to be careful."

"I will."

"And when the time comes, meet me here, and I will help you."

"What time?"

He did not look at me. "When next Cuffee gets in trouble and the King's men decide to burn your friend."

His bluntness terrified me. The very words seared me. "Burn? They won't burn anybody. They did that last time. It's barbaric, my mistress says. They won't do it again."

"They will do it," he said calmly. "And if it is someone you care about, then I can make it easier for them. If you come to me."

"For what?"

"A remedy I will give you for them to take so the flames don't hurt. The color of fire makes no difference if they do not suffer."

"A remedy?" I knew I sounded stupid.

"I can make it easier for them. So come to me."

"Suppose you're not here when that time comes?" I asked.

"I will be here. Remember."

I nodded yes, as if I understood. I shivered. I looked into his brown eyes. They seemed, one moment, to reflect the pond, and in the next to show me eternity. His eyes were old. He remembered things the rest of us didn't know about yet.

There was a reason the rich people in town all sent their slaves to purchase things from him. He had remedies no one else had. For burns, inside the body and out, for scars that wouldn't heal, inside and out, for loss of hair, for strength of teeth, for fevers and agues and chills and the maladies of old age.

He spoke now of none of these.

I did not know of what he now spoke, but it made me chilled to think on it. And then I asked. "Did you do this last time? For the others they burned?"

He knew what I meant. The year 1712. "I was a young man then," he said, "just starting out. And now I'm an old man and nothing has changed."

I asked him about some of the slaves who had escaped and were living with the Indians. He smiled and said they were doing well.

"Did you watch last time?" I asked him. "Did you watch the burnings?"

He said no. "I didn't have to. I heard the screams. From all but those I gave my potion to."

"Did you give it to Cuffee's father?"

He shook his head no. "His wife would not take it. So he burned."

"Why wouldn't she take it?"

"Ask her, why don't you?" And he laughed and gathered up his things. Then he said: "Tell your friend to mind himself. Then you won't have to make the decision."

"What decision?"

"The one your mind is wondering about now. The one Cuffee's mother could not make. Tell your friend to mind himself."

I promised him I would.

"Such a pretty girl," he said as I turned to leave. "Shouldn't have to be concerned with such things. But I knew your mother. She was pretty too. And she was always concerned. Blessings on you, child."

I looked at him. I wanted to ask him if Mr.

Ury was a priest. I wanted to ask if I would talk when the time came. I sensed he knew the answers to these questions. But I just turned and started back across the sand to my path in the woods. It was a long way back.

CHAPTER SEVEN

I RUSHED HOME, determined to get the medicines there safely. I knew how precious they were, and how they meant hours without pain for my mistress. And I didn't want to be on the streets, which weren't a safe place for a Negro to be anymore. Besides, I had lessons this afternoon with Mr. Ury.

Then, I met Mrs. Luckstead on Maiden Lane. She was carrying a basket too, only hers was bigger and heavier. She had been to market.

What mood would she be in? I wondered. Her regular, everyday mood? Or the mood in which she acted out witchcraft?

"Hello, Mrs. Luckstead," I said.

"The price of a good piece of mutton is unbelievable these days. Hello, Phoebe Philipse. Where are you rushing from?"

It was her regular everyday mood. Still, I did not want to say. I didn't bandy it about that I met with Doctor Harry, more to protect him than anything. I looked at her, at the scar on her face, near her nose.

It was general knowledge that she'd been captured by bad Indians as a child, but had escaped. She said they meant to cut off her nose, but missed. She gave them credit for her "powers." Some said the story was made up to make herself more intriguing. Others said no, she had been taken. Still others said it didn't matter anyway since she was crazy.

But I had always thought there was a measure of sanity in her that others did not give her credit for, so I listened to her when others laughed.

"The work at the tavern is endless since my son-in-law and daughter were put in prison," she said. "Not that they don't deserve to be there. I always told them that keeping stolen goods to resell was a bad business. They've started to call our tavern the Trappers' Rest, like the Indian trading post up north. How are you keeping, Phoebe?"

"As well as can be expected. Were they put in prison for keeping stolen goods? Or for the fire plot?"

"A little of both, I expect. I never liked my son-in-law. He was always looking for trouble. On an errand, are you?"

"Yes, ma'am."

"You're a good girl, Phoebe. How is your mistress?"

"She's keeping."

"Listen," she said, stepping closer and dropping her voice. "I want to speak to you as if you were my child." I nodded. "You have no one to advise you. So I will. Talk, if you are given the chance."

"Talk?"

"To the King's men. Talk and get your freedom."

"I don't have anything to say."

She scoffed. "We all do. We all know things. We have eyes and ears, don't we? There's nothing like freedom, child. Take it from somebody who was a prisoner when she was young. What's here for you, child? Get out of this town."

"And go where?"

"To the friendly Indians. Doctor Harry will help you when the time comes."

"What has Doctor Harry to do with it?"

"I know, I know, you must protect him. But just let him help you when the time comes."

"I truly have nothing to say," I told her.

"But you have the means of finding out."

"How?"

"Your Mr. Ury. They want to know if he's a priest as much as they want to know who set the fires. They fear he's at the crux of the revolt. They will continue to look, because they need a white man to blame, just as in the revolt of 1712."

"I couldn't do that to Mr. Ury, even if he was to blame."

"Don't be such a child. Do you want to burn in your bed this night?"

"No."

"Do you want your master or mistress to burn? They will, if this business isn't stopped."

"Maybe the fires weren't set."

"The King's men have proved arson. Why was the hay piled to the roof at Quick and

Vergereau's? Only, it isn't a question of why anymore, but who. Besides, they will find someone to blame. And it may be the wrong ones. Like last time."

"Last time?" I quickened. "Were you here?"

"I was very young, and it was right before I was taken. I saw people burned. I saw the wrong ones burned. Don't let that happen again. And tell Cuffee to stay inside. Tell him to stay away from Prince. They have their eyes on him because of his father."

"I will," I said. "Thank you, Mrs. Luckstead."

"Don't thank me unless you take my advice. Don't let them say you're part of it, too. All they need is one person to start talking."

"I can't talk to get my freedom. I wouldn't want it that way."

She leaned closer. "Decide where your freedom is," she said. "I thought it was here, so I ran from the Indians. I found out then that they were my best friends. I had my real freedom with them. Don't make the mistake I did. Decide where it is, then protect it."

And then she went off, trotting past me, gone from my sight in the next moment, as if she had never been.

CHAPTER EIGHT

WHEN MR. URY came that afternoon to tutor me, I did look at him in a different way. I could not help it.

Was he a priest? I watched him closely, as if his movements, the way he set down the books, the way he moved his hands, had anything to do with it.

I wondered about him now. What did a priest do? What kind of special powers did he have? What was he really thinking? I knew there were rumors in town of a priest going about and christening people in secret at night.

Would he christen a Negro if the Negro wanted it?

Mr. Ury gave me my lessons in the back parlor, which was decorated in lovely brown accents. And I tried to behave as always, but he sensed something was wrong with me and twice he scolded because I wasn't paying attention.

I paid no mind to the scolding, which normally would bring me to tears. I was so fascinated with watching him. Instead, I asked. "Mr. Ury, where did you grow up?"

It was unseemly to ask, I know. And I expected more scolding. Instead he sighed and leaned back in his chair.

"In England. My family was well-esteemed and very comfortable. Until twenty years ago, when the company my father was secretary in went into bankruptcy. The financial failure killed my father. After he died, a gentleman friend of my father's took me in and became my benefactor. I was educated at two universities. Later I wrote a book on church history, but King George the Second didn't like it, so I was put in the Tower."

"The Tower of London!" My eyes went wide.

"Yes." He grimaced. "But I was fortunate enough to have good friends who got me out, and I fled to America. I taught in Philadelphia for years before I came here."

There was quiet in the room. And then he said: "So now can we get back to our lessons?"

But when did you become a priest? I wanted to ask. Because I sensed he was not telling me the whole truth. I also wanted to ask him why he dressed always in black. He was a tall, thin man, with graceful hands, a head full of dark hair, a long nose, and deep eyes.

What did priests do when they weren't teaching little girls? Mary Burton said they forgave sins. How did a person forgive sins? Was there a kind of black magic to it? I wanted to ask him, oh so badly.

Was he in charge of the slaves who had set the fires? If, indeed, slaves had set the fires. How could he be involved in such a terrible thing and be here in our parlor, without so much as a telltale frown to give him away?

Instead, we talked about the trade between England and America that afternoon. We talked about the English admiral Edward Vernon and how he defeated the Spanish in the Caribbean. We agreed that it was a great victory.

There were more fires that night. We had scarce retired when the alarm went out. And the people's cries were so plaintive in the night.

"Fire! Fire!"

People came out of their houses in their nightclothes. It turned out the fire was across the river in New Jersey. Hackensack, somebody said.

You could see the orange-red flames eating up the darkness of the night sky.

My master told me to go back to bed, so I did. But first I looked to see if Cuffee was around. He was, standing there by the garden gate next to his mother, Old Rose. He nodded to me as I went by, his very presence giving me comfort. If I could only talk to him, I thought. He could make the world seem all right.

The next morning, word went through town that what had burned in New Jersey were barns. Seven of them had burned to the ground. The people came out to fight the fires, but soon two Negroes appeared with guns. That's what my master told us the next morning when he called us into the hallway.

"Negroes with guns." His voice sounded hollow, threatening, and frightened all at the same time. "One killed three white men. The other Negro shot his gun off but hit nobody, thank God. They were both soon apprehended. One confessed to setting fire to three barns. The other said nothing. Both are, as we speak, burning at the stake across the river. At least our friends in New Jersey know how to treat people who start fires."

I looked at Cuffee and he at me. He shook his head, ever so slightly. I knew what he would say. *He's not a mean man. He is frightened. They all are.*

"If any of you know anything about this, or any of our fires, I would advise you to talk," my master went on. "You can come to me first. You know what the rewards are. And while I hate to lose any of you, I'd be perfectly willing to give you your freedom in exchange for information."

Nobody spoke. He nodded, looked at the floor, said, "Well, then," and went back into the sun-filled dining room to have his breakfast.

* * *

Well, then.

"Master says I'm to go to market with you." Cuffee came over to me. "Says we should stay together. That way we can vouch for each other."

"What does that mean?"

"Means you can tell where I've been and I can tell where you've been."

He knew words that I didn't. I knew he read books, but he didn't talk much about that. I knew Cuffee talked about books sometimes with Mr. Ury when he came to tutor me.

We went to Coenties Market for fish for supper.

"Mary Burton is going to talk," I told him. "She's going to give King's evidence."

"Ten Negroes are in jail already. Isn't that enough?"

"They're letting them out."

"They're talking their way out, saying what the white man wants to hear. Quacko confessed to saying 'Fire, fire scorch, scorch a little, damn it, by and by,' but he said he was talking about our victories in the war with Spain and how wonderful they were. So they let him go, too. What is Mary going to talk about?"

"She says she knows things. About who plotted the fires. And if she doesn't, she'll make it up because she wants to end her indenture and get money."

"If she talks, she'll say who came to Hughson's. Who gathered there. And I'll be one of them. Mayhap I should run, Phoebe."

"No. If you run, they'll find you." I told him. "If you run, they'll say it's because you are guilty."

"And if I don't? I don't want to be like my father. He should have run."

I drew in my breath. It was the first time he'd ever spoken of his father to me. Was he opening doors to talk of him? What was he saying? What did he want me to say? I waited to see if he would talk any more about his father. He did.

"He should have run, my father. What worse could they have done to him but what they did? They burned him. It took him hours to die."

"Your mother—" I started to say, but he interrupted me.

"My mother was part to blame. She never gave him the decoction she was supposed to give."

"What was the decoction?" I asked.

He stopped. We were at the market now. I could smell the fish. "Poison," he said. "Poison that would kill him in minutes. If they sentence you to burn, you've got to have somebody to give it to you."

It came over me then like the smell of the fish. "Doctor Harry," I mumbled.

"What about Doctor Harry?"

I looked up into Cuffee's round, reassuring face. "He said I should go to him if they burned any of my friends. And he would give me something to give to them."

"Poison," he said.

We looked at each other.

"If they get me, Phoebe. If they take me and put blame on me and sentence me, you must go to Doctor Harry and get some."

"Cuffee, I can't give you poison," I said. The idea was so big, so black, that it came over me like a blanket, smothering me.

"You must. Don't be like my mother. She wouldn't do it for my father. And she wouldn't do it for me now. She says I have sins to make up for. You must do it for me, Phoebe. Promise."

Tears came to my eyes. I looked up at his dear face. "Cuffee," was all I could say. "Promise me you won't see Prince anymore. Prince is trouble."

"He's got a right to his anger," he said. "The governor won't let him see his wife. He loves his wife. I don't blame him for his anger. Suppose you were my wife?"

I blushed, but the thought alone pleased me.

"I'd want to see you." There was tenderness in his voice. I was only fourteen, but don't think I didn't pay mind to it sometimes.

"You must promise me, Phoebe," he said again, "to do what I ask. You're the only one I can trust. Promise."

So I promised him, to satisfy him. I promised him, to keep him quiet. I couldn't wrap my mind around the whole business now. My mind wasn't big enough. I needed time.

We bought the fish and went home as if we had no more to worry about this day. But who would clean it? Agnes wouldn't, so I knew the job would fall to Cuffee and he'd do it cheerfully. *He'd cook it for his master too*, I thought, *if asked.* There were a lot of dishes he cooked for his master because only he knew how. And it made Agnes jealous. She hated him.

I walked in silence, my feelings as dead as the fish he carried.

CHAPTER NINE

E ARRIVED HOME to find a crowd of about a dozen people, men and women, in front of our house.

One man saw us first and yelled: "Here he comes. With the girl."

I felt Cuffee quicken beside me and grabbed on to his sleeve. "Don't run," I whispered. "That's what they want you to do. Hold fast."

He did. And the crowd came at us like one

person. "You walk free because your owner is an assemblyman," one man accused. "You and that friend of yours. Prince."

"Well," another man took up, "we've decided that the Negroes are to blame for the fires."

"Yes, there are too many of you," a woman added. "And you have too much liberty. And something must be done."

"We want results," the first man put in. "We want more arrests and we want them now."

I could feel the heat of their anger, their desire for vengeance, their fear. And I measured that fear against my own and decided mine was greater. Then, just as they started toward us, a voice came from the side of the house.

"What you doin' out there, Cuffee? How many times I gotta tell you to stay off the streets?"

She held a pine torch. She was old and decrepit. Her gray hair was done up in a bun behind her head. Her face had lines like the cracks in the ice of the Hudson River in midwinter. She lived in a shack in back of the house, and seldom came out except to tend her garden of herbs. She had five cats.

She was Cuffee's mother, Old Rose. I didn't know much about her; I didn't ever speak to her.

Like most other people in the house and out of it, I was afraid of her.

I had only just found out the story about her husband in the last riot. But everybody, it seemed, knew this was the woman who'd held her babe in her arms and stood and watched while her husband was slow burned. Everybody, even those who hadn't been around then, felt responsible for it, because it was such a horrible death in comparison to hanging.

She, in turn, seldom spoke to anybody. Had no remorse.

"It's Old Rose," I heard one man whisper. "Be careful."

Now she looked at Cuffee. "Come here, son," she said.

He went to her. She reached up a scrawny hand and slapped his face. "I told you not to go about, didn't I?"

Cuffee never flinched.

"Now, go on in the house, 'fore you end up like your father."

Cuffee went. I stood alone. "You," she gestured to me, "you get yourself in here too."

I didn't know which was worse. Going to Old Rose or staying where I was. But I went to her. "Little black girl ain't got no more sense than a hooty owl," she said to me, and she pushed me toward the back door. "Go on, get outta my sight."

I ran, just as the front door opened and Mr. Philipse came out. "What's all this commotion out here?" he asked.

Seeing someone they could finally confront, the crowd turned to him, all talking at once.

Thank heaven for Old Rose, I thought, inside the house. Thank heaven people are afraid of her.

Mary Burton talked. She talked all they wanted, to the King's men. Cuffee and I were allowed to go to City Hall, to the gallery where the Negroes sat, to hear the proceedings. Mr. Ury went with us.

He had to sit downstairs with the white people, though he much preferred to sit with us.

I thought how small Mary looked down there on the witness stand. She wore her best blue. Only I knew the skirt was patched at the hem. It didn't show, and her apron and neckerchief were as white as could be.

At first she refused to talk. She refused even

to come to City Hall. "I'll not be sworn or give evidence," she said to the messenger.

When he again returned it was with orders to take her to jail if she wouldn't come. I think she intended to come all along and just didn't want it to look as though she were going to talk against her neighbors and friends.

On the witness stand she hesitated. She wouldn't respond to questions at the outset, but they kept at her.

"Tell us what you know of the fires. Of the robbery at Hogg's shoppe."

It was from Hogg's shoppe that the things had been taken that ended up at Hughson's tavern, to be sold later.

There were seventeen men staring at her, waiting for her reply, threatening to jail her if she didn't come out with an answer.

How would I act if I were her?

They read to her about the rewards for talking. They spoke of the money she would get, the freedom from indenture, the protection.

"She's frightened," I whispered to Cuffee.

"That girl about as scared as a water moccasin," he said.

And he was right. For then she opened her mouth and the words spewed out. I heard Cuffee give a low moan.

"I've heard Negroes plotting to burn the city at Hughson's tavern," she told the King's men. "I know the Hughsons received stolen goods to resell and make a profit."

"Tell us about the fires," they insisted.

She was fearful until they said that if she didn't, the most damnable sin would lie at her door. Then she spoke. "I've heard Caesar, Prince, and Cuffee plotting to burn the fort to the ground. They talked about burning the whole town. Then Caesar would be governor and Hughson, my master, would be king."

I heard Cuffee swear under his breath. I saw his hands clench in his lap. I knew that Negroes were not allowed anyone to defend them if put on trial. I prayed they would not arrest him then and there, but they were too intrigued by what Mary was saying.

"My master and mistress said they'd assist the Negroes. Caesar, Prince, and Cuffee said they would set the fires at night and when the people came out to fight them, they'd shoot them dead. I know my master and mistress have guns enough for all. They said that if I ever made mention of this, they'd poison me. The Negroes said that if I made bad talk about them, they'd burn me."

Cuffee got up and left the gallery. I followed. Outside we stood in the beautiful spring weather and just looked at each other.

"They'll come for me," he said.

"It's only one girl's talk. They won't believe her."

"They will, because they want to," he said.

Mr. Ury came out of City Hall and over to us. "Mayhap you should think of leaving, Cuffee," he said. "You'll get no fair shake in there."

"Where will he go?" I asked.

My teacher just looked at me. "He knows where to go if he has to."

"Doctor Harry?" I looked at Cuffee and he gave me a half nod. "The Senecas would take me in. But I only go with Prince. I can't leave my friend Prince."

But it turned out that Prince didn't want to go. His wife was sick and the governor still wouldn't let him see her.

My master sent a note around to the

governor to ask him to allow Prince to see her. Sometimes I think there was nothing my master wouldn't do for Cuffee, and I wondered how Cuffee felt, knowing he was planning on running away.

Over the next few days, nothing happened. And then I was preparing for bed in my little room on the third floor when I heard a great commotion on the grounds outside. The peacocks that my master used as watch birds were making enough noise to make us think the Spanish were finally attacking.

I went downstairs and followed Agnes outside. There stood three magistrates with Cuffee in tow. His hands were tied behind his back. He was wearing his blue coat with the red silk lining, and it and the rest of his clothing were askew. His head was bowed.

My master stood just outside the back door. "He's the best servant I've ever had," I heard him say. "There is no one more loyal."

"He was caught with a pine-knot torch, about to set fire to the governor's house. Him and that friend of his, Prince," one magistrate said.

"He was visiting the governor's house with

his friend Prince, whose wife works there," my master explained. But they did not listen to him.

In back of them I saw Old Rose come out of her shack, a shawl wrapped around her thin frame. She did not look at the men or even at Cuffee.

She looked at me.

They hauled Cuffee off. He stumbled once, but they righted him. "Wasn't gonna burn no house. The torch was for light," he said. "Just wanted to help Prince see his woman. It's not right he can't see her and her ailin' so. Not right."

"Courage, Cuffee!" my master called out. But he did not go with them. I thought at least he would go upstairs and put on his best breeches and shirt and good coat and go with them.

They made new rules the next day that forbade Negroes to carry torches. And they made a curfew. Negroes were to be off the streets at seven at night.

"It's like the witch trials up in Salem forty-some years back," Mr. Ury told me when he came for my lessons. "Talk and they love you. Name more names of innocent people and they love you and let you go free. Plead innocence and you are in jail."

I think he was wondering what names Cuffee would give them. And if one would be his own.

CHAPTER TEN

*I*T WAS IMPOSSIBLE to believe. They had Cuffee. My thoughts went around in circles, starting at one point and coming back to it in the end. Cuffee was in jail. Would they put him on trial? Would they ask him to talk against his friends? I knew Cuffee would never do that. He'd die first.

From there my mind went right to what I was supposed to do if they decided to execute him. I knew I could not give him poison. In that way I was like Old Rose. How could you give poison to someone you loved?

And then I'd ask myself, *Why me?* Why not someone else? Why had Cuffee asked me to give him poison if they were to burn him?

Because he could trust me, was why.

Don't trust me, I wanted to say. I could not poison my friend. Besides, it was wrong, wasn't it? Wouldn't God strike me dead for doing it? That was it. God. I was more than sure it was something He wouldn't countenance.

But how could I be sure? It came to me then that I didn't know about God except as someone we prayed to in our Anglican church on Sundays. According to Master, He was an ever-present Presence, who looked over our shoulders all day. But somehow I couldn't perceive Him now that I needed him.

And then I knew. I'd ask Mr. Ury. If he were truly a priest, he would know. But first then, I must ask him. Did I have the courage to do that?

"Your answers are wrong here, Phoebe. I thought you understood subtraction."

I watched him from across the room. I watched the way he moved, the sureness of him, the way he was so unafraid, the gestures he made with his hands as he held my papers. He looked at me.

"These sums are wrong. What is it? Surely you understand by now."

"I worry for Cuffee," I said.

"So do we all." He dropped his gaze.

"Suppose they put him to death?"

He did not answer right off. He shrugged. "It is appointed that all men must die," he said.

I huddled in the chair, pushing myself into it as far as I could. "He wants me to poison him if they are to burn him," I said quietly. "He wants me to get a remedy from Doctor Harry and give it to him."

"And what did you say?" he asked.

"I made no promise. I just listened."

"And now you want to know if it's the right thing to do, is that it?"

I nodded yes.

"Why ask me? Why not his mother? Why not your master? They both hold him in high esteem."

"Because of who you are," I said quietly.

"I'm a wandering teacher." I vigorously shook my head no. "Then who am I?" he asked.

"Everybody says you're a priest."

He looked at me long and hard. His brown eyes bore into me. "Do they, now?"

"Yes. And they say you can forgive sins. And if you can do that, then you know what sins are. And you can tell me if it be a sin if I do this."

"You worry about the rightness of it," he said.

"I worry more because I don't think I have the courage to do it. So I thought I'd blame it on God," I said.

He smiled. "Your honesty is like a breath of fresh air, Phoebe. I wish more people had it. You are truly in a dilemma here. And if I were a priest I would have to say that it isn't ours to interfere in the way someone dies. That you'd be playing God."

"So? Are you, then?"

"Would that same honesty lead you to running around and telling everybody?"

"No. I'd keep your secret."

He nodded. "I believe you would. Yes, I am."

"And you can forgive sins? Like Mary Burton says?"

"So that's what she says. That girl has too much to say, if you ask me. But yes, I can."

I leaned forward. "How do you do it?"

"Do what?"

"Forgive sins."

He smiled. "A special power was given to me."

"What else can you do?"

He scowled. "I can make little girls study so they'll do their sums right. Really now, Phoebe, we must get back to work. Your master is paying me."

"But what do you have to say about me and Cuffee?"

"I'd say do what is in your heart."

He would say no more. And so we got back to work. But I looked at him in a different way now. When we were finished I said, "I would like to see you do something special. Could I?"

He thought for a moment. "I'm christening a baby tonight. At the Arnold house. The baby has been ill and they want it christened in case it dies. You can come with me if you wish. But I must swear you to secrecy."

"I'm a slave," I said. "I'm not allowed out on the streets past curfew."

"Oh, yes. Well, if you're with me it'll be all right. I'll ask your master to write you a pass."

And so it was agreed. I would go with him tonight.

CHAPTER ELEVEN

*M*R. URY ASKED my master if he could have me on loan to help at a supper party at the Arnolds', who were friends of his. Sometimes wealthy people hired out their Negro servants. But tonight it wasn't for the money I would earn. It was simply a matter of Mr. Philipse helping a friend.

My master often hired me out for such duty. Going into other people's houses I always saw and learned a lot. And I was never overworked, but treated kindly, because I belonged to Mr. Philipse.

I wondered, going over and over things in my mind, did Master know Mr. Ury was a priest? Was that why he'd given him the job of tutoring me? To help him earn money? My master was not Catholic. We went to Trinity Church, where all the important people went.

That night I found it difficult to keep stride with Mr. Ury as we went along the path to our destination, which was on Dock Street, on the East River. Here was a whole strip of houses owned by wealthy men.

"The house is all lighted," I said. "Candles in every window."

"There are reasons for that," Mr. Ury told me. "First, it doesn't look as if anything secretive is going on, and second, they can afford it. Mr. Arnold made his money from shipping grain to the West Indies, like so many others here in the city. But many have lost profits from both growing Hudson Valley wheat and shipping it, of late. Philadelphia and Baltimore are giving them competition, and falling profits mean lost wages for many. There's a mathematics problem for you, Phoebe. The answer to that problem is that New

Yorkers are looking for somebody to blame for things going bad financially. So, as always, they're blaming the Negro, because so many Negroes are living well here."

He made a lesson out of everything, Mr. Ury did.

The house was three stories high and richly appointed, outside and in. We went in the front way. He went up the stone steps and pounded the brass knocker, bold as anything, and a maid let us in.

I thought she would send me to the kitchen to be with the other slaves, but Mr. Ury bade me carry his leather pouch and assist him. I'd been instructed what to do. I was to hand him the ingredients for the christening as he asked for them.

The first thing I heard was a baby crying. It was a cry filled with distress.

We went into the parlor, where a pewter punch bowl sat on the table. It was empty. Mr. and Mrs. Arnold came in, and Mr. Arnold shook Mr. Ury's hand. Mrs. Arnold held the baby close to her. Its cry subsided somewhat, but still I could see the baby was not well. It was richly done up in white clothing. Mrs. Arnold handed it to Mr. Ury. He took it and held it tenderly and blessed it, then handed it to another woman who stepped close to the table.

Mr. Ury asked me for the bottle of water from the leather pouch, and I gave it to him. He poured it into the punch bowl. It wasn't much, but it was holy, the label said.

It didn't look any different from any other water, far as I could see.

I stood just behind Mr. Ury for the whole thing. I saw the lady friend hold the baby over the punch bowl. I heard him mumble prayers in some special tongue, then pour the holy water over the baby's head. I handed him the holy oil when he asked for it. I saw the faces of the people crowded around. Mrs. Arnold was crying.

The baby was a boy and they christened him David.

Now he was sleeping, and Mrs. Arnold clasped her hands in front of her as she beheld this. And when it was done Mr. Ury turned to her. "I've done my best," he said. "The rest is up to God."

She thanked him profusely and took her baby back. "Please, stay and have some refreshment," she begged.

Afterward, though I helped serve supper and was in and out of the dining room frequently, I never saw her put that baby down all night.

As we left, Mr. Arnold paid Mr. Ury for my services. "Let me know," Mr. Ury said. "Send word. You should know by morning."

"Know what?" I asked him on the walk home."

"If the fever breaks. The child was so hot. Either the fever will break by morning or it will die. Sometimes baptism helps them."

"You mean because you christened that baby it might live?"

He shrugged. "Sometimes it happens," he said.

CHAPTER TWELVE

*T*HE NIGHT WAS clear, with a crescent moon, and the stars hung low over the Hudson River. When we got to Mr. Philipse's house, Mr. Ury bade me good night.

"Do you do much of what you did tonight?" I asked him at the door.

"I do a share of it."

So. There were lots of Catholics in New York, then. "If they find out about you . . ." My voice stopped.

"They won't. Unless somebody talks," he said.

"Why do they hate Catholics so much?"

"Why does any group of people hate another, Phoebe? Because they misjudge the ones they hate. Because they don't really know them."

I nodded. "Do you think your magic will work with the baby?"

"It isn't magic, Phoebe. It's faith. And if nothing else, it took away his sin."

"How can he have sin?"

"We're born with it. All of us."

"And if you're not christened, it doesn't go away?"

"That's what we believe, yes."

"Even Negroes?"

"Yes."

"Then I already have sin. So giving Cuffee poison wouldn't be any worse than what I was born with."

He shook his head. "It doesn't work that way, Phoebe."

"How does it work, then?"

"It's too late to explain it now."

"What should I do, then, Mr. Ury? Tell me."

"I told you. Listen to your heart, Phoebe. But I'll tell you one thing you should do. Go and visit Mary Burton. Where are they keeping her?"

"In City Hall."

"Go and visit her. Try to get her to recant her testimony."

"What does that mean?"

"Take it back. Change it. Only she can save Cuffee now. And you're friends with her. That's what I'd tell you to do."

And with that he disappeared into the night, with his leather pouch and the magic that was in it.

The next morning a young Negro came to the door with a note for me. She was from the Arnolds. The note said they did not know where Mr. Ury lived. But that the Arnold baby lived, and it had no more fever.

I went to see Mary Burton in her little whitewashed room at City Hall. I brought a basket of fresh bread and fruit and cheese. She eyed it hungrily. "How nice of you to come."

We sat at a small table and she ate. "Is the tavern being kept up?" she asked.

I told her about Mrs. Luckstead and how she was running it with Peggy, their other indentured servant girl. "But Mrs. Luckstead complains of the work," I said.

"She always complains of the work. She doesn't like to do anything but conjure. A lot of good it does her."

I thought of Mr. Ury and his conjuring. And the baby. But I said nothing about it to her. I knew better than to tell her anything like that.

"Anyway, I'm going to be out of here soon," she told me. "And when I get out, I'll be free of my indenture. Free, Phoebe, just like I said. They will keep their promise, you'll see. They've offered me money too. I told you I would get money."

I nodded. "Is it worth it to you?"

"Now, don't get uppity, Phoebe."

"You betrayed your friends."

"I told the truth. I told them Mr. Roosevelt's Quacko was a friend of Caesar, Cuffee, and Prince. I told them Mr. Sleydell's Jack had secrets with Hughson and his wife."

"You've damned them all," I said.

"All of what I said is true."

"Cuffee is in jail now."

"Is that my fault?"

"No. But if you took back what you said about him, it could help. If you don't, they'll likely put him to death."

"Look here, Phoebe. I didn't do the things Cuffee and his friends did."

"They didn't set the fires."

"Well, they were running around having sport while I was slaving away in that tavern."

"You envy the slaves their free time?"

"They have too much of it. It's what brought on trouble. I'm white and indentured and I didn't have it by half."

"Don't you care about Cuffee, Mary?"

"I care about me, Mary Burton, who's been a workhorse since she got to this country. I tell you, if I'd known how hard it was here I'd have stayed back in England. Well, I've been given a way out now, and I'd be a fool not to take it. And you'll be a fool too, if you don't take it when the time comes, Phoebe."

"What time? Did you say things about me?"

She rolled her eyes. "No, but that doesn't mean they won't want to talk to you. Stop being a little fool. If you don't think of yourself, nobody will."

I quickened with fear. What else had she told the King's men that would bring people to ruin? I dared not ask. I was trembling when I left. She thanked me for the repast, and I didn't even say "You're welcome."

CHAPTER THIRTEEN

*T*HAT NIGHT Ben Thompson's house burned down. And the next morning smoke was pouring out of the windows of the house of attorney Joseph Murray, Esquire. The town was in a frenzy once again.

I was almost ashamed of myself, I was so glad Cuffee was in jail. At least they couldn't pin these fires on him.

People were running in the streets when I left the house. I had just persuaded Mr. Philipse to allow me to go out. I was going to visit Cuffee.

I had money with me. I had been advised by Mr. Ury that I might have to bribe a guard to see Cuffee in jail. The money I had was from my own little private store. I'd polished many a lady's shoes and pressed many men's coats while they visited to earn myself shillings.

"Can't see him. Orders," the guard said to me. Just as I expected he would.

And when I dug into my basket and retrieved the shillings and handed them out, he said nothing, but let me through.

Negroes were imprisoned underground in City Hall and it was nothing if not dank and chilly down there, in spite of the warm spring day outside. I found Cuffee in an end cell. He looked like a kicked puppy dog, cowering in the corner.

"Cuff."

"Phoebe. What you doin' here?" But he was delighted to see me. And even more delighted when I gave him the bread and cheese and fruit I'd saved for him.

From outside his cell, I watched him eat, watched the familiar motions as if I'd never seen them before. "How's my mama takin' all this, Phoebe?"

"Not good," I told him. "I saw her talking to the master in the yard this morning. I got the feeling they were talking about you."

He nodded. "She's asking him to come and testify for me. I know it."

"He said he wouldn't, Cuff. You know he said he wouldn't do it again."

"Yeah, I know." He continued eating. "Know what they said to me? They said if I speak the truth, the governor will pardon me even if I was in the plot. Know what I said?"

"What?"

"That's what they told the Negroes last time. In 1712."

"And what did they answer?"

"They just huffed and puffed. Like they always do. You see, I know, Phoebe, I know who talked about fire and who didn't. But I'm not gonna tell. They can burn me, an' I won't tell."

I wanted to ask him, oh, how badly I wanted to ask him. *Did you talk about fire? Is there a plot?* But I could not do it. I did not want the knowledge of it inside me, in case I would be questioned.

As I left, he grabbed my hand through his

cell bars and told me not to worry, and to give his mother his best. "An' you remember," he said, "to get that remedy from Doctor Harry if I need it."

I said yes, I would. Oh, God help me, I said yes.

Monday morning, when I told Mr. Ury about the Arnold baby being well, all he said was, "Good, good."

I wanted to talk about it. He didn't. All he wanted to talk about was how New York City came to be divided into seven wards.

"Will the baby stay well?" I asked him.

"As well as any baby. Now tell me, when did the Dutch hand over New York to the English?"

"I went to City Hall," I said.

Now he was interested. His black eyebrows went up. "And, what did she say? Is she willing to recant any of her testimony?"

"No, sir. All she wants is to be free. And to have money. And she's angry at the Negroes because some of us haven't worked as hard as she. She said she'd never have come here if she knew how hard she'd have to work."

He sighed. "Most of us wouldn't," he said.

Most of the Negroes who had been jailed had been let out because their masters came to testify for them. So now the public was crying for justice. The King's men knew it.

The only Negroes they still had in jail were Prince, Caesar, and Cuffee. They had trials, but Negroes were not allowed to take an oath, so they couldn't defend themselves. Someone would have to step forward and be a character witness for them.

I decided to approach my master and ask him if he would be a character witness for Cuffee.

He was in his library. The windows were open to the early May evening. From outside came the twittering of birds, and I even caught a glimpse of orange tulips in the side garden.

He glowered at me over his desk. "You dare ask me that, Phoebe? Didn't I save him once already?"

"Yes, sir."

"And didn't I warn all of you that I wouldn't do it again?"

I said "Yes, sir" to that, too, and crept from the room. I was a coward, is what I was. But

I just never could abide it when my master scolded me.

On May the eighth, a verdict of guilty was given for Caesar and Prince. On the eleventh, they were hanged, and afterward, they fixed Caesar's corpse, in chains, on a platform near the city's powder house.

"You have to give the people justice or they will rise up themselves," I heard my master mutter as he stood gazing out the parlor window. "The people are frightened, hungry for justice."

I knew he meant the white people. I stood in the hallway. There was no one in the room with my master, and I wondered if he was frightened himself.

My mistress was not always in full possession of her mind. She had what my master called "lapses." When she had these lapses, she had trouble figuring out who everybody was and what was going on in the world around her.

I knew by now that my master had brought me into the house to act as a buffer between my mistress and the cruelties of the world.

"I don't want her to know any bad news,"

he told me once. "I want her life to be happy."

"But what if she asks?" I'd said.

And he had turned to me and spoken plain. "Then you lie," he told me. "She has no way of finding out the truth."

Now it appeared that one of the servants, likely Old Rose, had slipped into the house and talked in front of her about Caesar's body hanging in chains. "Is it true," she asked when I brought her breakfast one morning, "that Caesar's body is hanging near the powder house? Why is it hanging? Did he kill himself?"

In her eyes there was an intelligent light. There was no lapse now. Nor was there any pain in her hands or in her joints. "It's just one of those stories that go around in the slave community every so often, Mistress," I told her. "There is no truth in it. You know we Negroes love to keep ourselves amused with stories like that."

"You're no ordinary Negro, Phoebe," she said. "You're my own Phoebe." And she took my hand in her own. And I wondered, *What will she say if they put Cuffee to death? How can I tell her?* She had a special fondness for Cuffee. She was fond of saying she had raised him at her knee.

More to the point, I thought, how can I keep it from her? Old Rose would surely tell somehow, if only to make someone else share the pain she had suffered all her life.

CHAPTER FOURTEEN

I WANTED TO go visit Cuffee in jail again, but first I had to ask my master.

He was just finishing his breakfast. He ate alone at the dining room table for all his meals, since, except on rare occasions when Cuffee carried her in her chair downstairs, his wife took hers upstairs in her room. Sometimes a guest would stop in for breakfast with my master, but I made sure he was alone before presenting myself.

"Master, I'd like to visit Cuffee today. May I?"

He was sipping the last of his tea and reading the newspaper. "Didn't you just visit?"

"Yes, sir."

"Then why again so soon?"

"I'm afraid he's lonely, sir."

"That is the whole point in being jailed."

"I've had news from people that all he does is read or cry."

"There isn't much else to do in prison, is there?"

I know he was angry because Cuffee had gotten into trouble again. I did not answer. He shook the newspaper in front of him and glared at me over the top of it.

"People will start to think you're involved in the plot, you going there to see him so much."

"I was only there once, sir."

"Don't sass me. That's once too much."

"But I have all these things in my basket for him. Everybody is sending something. Good cornbread, and a book to read, and clean hose."

He just humphed. "Have you done all your chores already?"

"I brought breakfast to the mistress, fed the chickens, and made my bed. I could be back by the noon meal to sit with Mistress. And read to her."

He gave out a big sigh. "You're spoiled, all of you. Too much time on your hands."

"Yes, sir," I said.

"Doesn't Mr. Ury come today?"

"He comes every day, sir."

"I said don't sass me."

I fell silent. I knew his moods, and the best I could do with this one was keep a still tongue in my head. So I just stood there, shifting my weight from one foot to the other and holding my basket, while he read.

Finally he looked up. "You still here?"

"I'm waiting for permission, sir."

"Go, go." He waved his hand in disgust.

"Do you have any message for Cuffee, sir?" I knew I was pushing it, but it would do Cuffee so much good if the master sent an encouraging word.

"Tell the scoundrel he's well served, being in prison. And tell him—" He hesitated. I waited. "Tell him when he goes to trial I'll be a character witness. But that's all I'll do. He's on his own now."

"Yes, sir." I ran out the back door into the

lovely May morning. It wasn't a lot, his being a character witness. But it was something, anyway. And Mr. Ury had told me why Mr. Philipse would not step forward now and do more. Because he wanted to be counted as standing with his important friends, and not against them. He was someone to be reckoned with in the community.

If I were someone to be reckoned with, I'd stand up for my own people, I thought.

Below ground, where the Negro prisoners were housed, water ran down the walls, and it was so dark you needed candles to make your way through the dank halls.

I felt a sense of urgency. Cuffee must be in a state now that they hanged Caesar and Prince. It came to me that I'd never seen him cry.

The first thing I noticed was that his shoulders were slumped. He was half turned away from me, as if not wanting to look right in my face.

"What's wrong, Cuffee?" I asked.

He shrugged. "Nothing."

"I know it's terrible, what's happened."

"Terrible?" His voice was hard. "They didn't even give 'em a chance."

"Well, you'll have your chance. Master won't let them treat you like that."

"It's more than that."

"Tell me."

"I made a bad mistake, Phoebe. I just about hanged myself."

"How?" Panic rose in my throat.

"Yesterday they put Arthur Price in this cell with me."

Arthur Price was a white man, an indentured servant whose master was the merchant Captain Vincent Pearse. He'd been jailed for taking things from the fort after it was burned.

"Why did they do that? White people's cells are upstairs."

"I was stupid, is what happened. Should have thought he wanted to make good for himself with the King's men. Should have known he'd talk, like Mary Burton, to get out of here. The jailer gave us each a tankard of punch to make us feel better. Trouble is, it loosed my tongue and I told Price things I shouldn't have."

"What did you tell him?"

"That I was sworn by Hughson not to tell of plans for the fires."

"Oh, Cuffee!"

"Yeah," he said dolefully. "And that Mr. Roosevelt's Quacko had been in on the fire at Fort George. Because he was. Right after that they took Price out of here. I think I done myself in, Phoebe. But I think I did Quacko in more. And that's why I've been crying. If Quacko hangs, it'll be my fault. I'm scared."

"Likely Quacko's name has been given already by Mary," I said, for lack of anything else to say. I knew how bad he must feel, and I had no answers for him.

And then he asked, in the tone of a child, "Phoebe, how come you never asked me if I set any fires?"

"Because," I said, "knowing of the plans and being part of them yourself are two different things."

"You're a good girl, Phoebe."

"Master sends his best," I lied.

A hopeful look came into his eyes. "He do?"

"Yes, and he told me to tell you that when you go on trial he'll be a character witness."

His face brightened. "That'll be all I need then, won't it, Phoebe? He's a 'portant man. His word will count, won't it?"

Again I had no answer for him. And I still did not ask him if he had been in on the fires. I did not want to know.

After I left Cuffee, I went upstairs and slipped into the back of the courtroom and stood behind a pillar so nobody would see me. I half believed what my master had said, that if they saw me loitering about they might call on me to testify.

The courtroom itself was frightening. It had a peaked ceiling and great windows framed in oak. It reminded me of the inside of Trinity Church.

Words echoed in here and carried on the air as true. The voices of the King's men were loud, and they walked back and forth waving their arms while they questioned the poor soul sitting there. I imagined that this is what it would be like on Judgment Day when God questioned us about our sins.

Mary Burton was testifying, naming names as fast as she could think of them.

She too said Mr. Roosevelt's Quacko was in on the fires. And Mr. Sleydell's Jack. And Mr. Vaarck's Jonneau. And Mistress Carpenter's Albany.

She named thirty Negroes in all who came to

Hughson's tavern and plotted to make fires in the city and murder the white inhabitants.

I did not know what the truth of this was. I did not know if anybody knew the truth anymore, if anybody knew who had really set the fires. Or if the King's men even cared, as long as they had somebody to blame.

But I did know that Mary was lying.

I had never seen some of these Negroes in the tavern, for all my visiting there to get my master's dram. *How could she do this?* I wondered. *How could she lie like this?* For I knew it was lies. One or two Negroes might have said something in jest while at the tavern, and Mary was turning it into a plot.

She was still talking when I left. I had to get back to give my mistress her noon meal.

I heard later that every time a Negro was brought in they were told what Cuffee had been told, that if they named names they would go free.

Most did not talk. But Mr. Niblet's Sandy spoke enough for all of them, naming names, telling who had set fire to what, and telling who was to be captain of what Negro company, and who was to be a soldier.

This last threw the King's men into a frenzy. The Negroes had formed military companies!

"Mr. McMullen's Augustine said he'd burn his master's house. He was to have been an officer," Sandy said.

The Negroes had two military companies, it seemed. The Fly Company and the Long Bridge Company.

The King's men decided that it must be stopped. Another warning must be given.

They must have another execution.

CHAPTER FIFTEEN

I PROBABLY WOULD never have gotten to the trial for Cuffee and Quacko if Mr. Ury hadn't spoken for me. On Monday, during lessons, he noticed that my spirits had been brought low, and asked why. I told him I was worried about both Quacko and Cuffee, and wanted to go to the trial, which began on the morrow. But Master didn't want me near the court anymore.

"He thinks if the King's men see me, they'll

be reminded that I know Cuffee, and make me testify," I said.

He answered with a peculiar thought then, but one that was just like him: "The Kings's men don't have to see you, Phoebe. Or me. They know us all. We can hide nothing," he said. And then: "Look here, I'll take you. I'll tell your master it's a perfect example of our judicial system and you can learn, firsthand, what it's like, seeing the Supreme Court in action."

And so I went to City Hall with Mr. Ury. I felt important accompanying him. On the street some people nodded hello. Others turned away. I supposed that those who turned away thought he was a Catholic priest.

Once inside City Hall, however, we had to separate. Though hated as a suspected priest, he was allowed to sit downstairs. Because I was Negro, I had to go up to the gallery. I didn't mind. You could really see better from up there. I found a seat and waited for court to begin.

It mattered little that I knew the judge, Daniel Horsmanden, Esquire, that I'd served at special dinners at his house, that I knew he liked his rum, and that I'd seen him grab his housemaid around the waist in the hall and plant a kiss on her lips. He looked like God just then. And if the black robes and white wig he and the other four lawyers wore were meant to frighten, they did the trick.

They brought Quacko and Cuffee in, and I thought how ragged they looked in their old dirty clothing. And how my mistress would be ashamed for Cuffee just now and would have sent a clean shirt if she'd been herself these last two days.

They seemed befuddled by it all, their surroundings and the people who were sitting there staring at them. I wanted to call out to Cuffee, to show him I was here, but of course I dared not. I dared not even wave.

There was a prayer to begin with. Then somebody boomed that God should save the King and the great province of New York. Then there was a lot of legal talk that I did not understand. These people seemed to have a language all their own. It's another way of seeming to have power, I thought, having a language all your own.

I learned more that morning than I had in the last six months with Mr. Ury. Some of it I couldn't grasp, of course, but all I had to do was look at the faces of Cuffee and Quacko to know that the facts and the lies and the half lies were stacked against them. And that they knew it.

White people got up there and told the lawyers how they'd seen Cuffee and Quacko here and they'd seen them there.

"I saw them at the fort just before the fire," said Mr. Vreeland, who owned a green grocery store.

"Of course I saw them," Mr. Martin vowed. "At Abraham Kipp's brewhouse, and at Mr. Philipse's warehouse at the bucket brigade. I saw Cuffee refuse to take part."

Arthur Price got up there, he who had been in Cuffee's cell with him yesterday. He was all spiffed up to look like a model citizen. "I know I took things from the fort after it burned," he admitted, "but nohow was I part of the fires. In his cell yesterday Cuffee told me he was sworn by Hughson not to tell of plans for the fires."

Well, I thought, he'll not only get out of jail for this, he'll get out of his indenture.

Cuffee and Quacko were allowed to call for ten witnesses to say good things about them. I near lost my breath when my master took the stand.

There was dead silence in the courtroom. Master would not look at Cuffee and I knew, right off, that something was wrong. But he told how good a servant he was. "Faithful and true," he said.

"Was he home the nights of the fires?" he was asked.

"He knows just how hot I like my water for shaving," came the reply.

The judge leaned forward. "The night of the fires. Was he home?"

"He sews the buttons on my jacket when they come loose." Master looked out over the courtroom as if he were home in his study. "He makes blueberry grunt for me in the summer because nobody else can do it as he can. He makes me laugh when my spirits are down."

The courtroom went silent before it broke out into a low rumble of conversation. The judge banged his gavel. "I will have quiet," he said. I saw Cuffee bow his head. I heard my own heart beat. Master would not testify for Cuffee! Was it because he would not lie? Or because he was afraid of the censure of his friends?

But we both knew that Cuffee had been

home for most of the nights of the fires. Why did he not explain?

Was it because if Cuffee was out even one night of the fires, he would be accused of taking part in them?

And then lawyer William Smith got up there and broke the whole mood.

"These Negroes can sew on all the buttons they want," he said. "When they aren't doing that or making blueberry grunt they are in the act of making a revolution. They want money, power, and white women. When the time comes, they will plunder the wealth of their slaughtered masters."

The room shook with his words.

He called them villains, beasts, and ungrateful monsters. He said more words I did not understand like "a presumption of guilt" and the "inherent dangers that slaves posed."

And then he said the one thing I hoped he wouldn't say. He talked about the slave revolt of 1712 and how Cuffee's father had been one of the leaders.

He talked about "innocent blood flowing in the streets" and "ridding the country of this vermin forever."

Cuffee and Quacko seemed to melt back into their chairs as he said all these terrible things. They kept getting smaller and smaller.

And then lawyer William Smith thanked Providence personally that the Negroes' "treacherous villainies" had been discovered, 'fore the town lay in ashes. And then he looked at Cuffee and Quacko. "Confess," he shouted, "and save yourselves from the fires of hell."

And then he said, "Each of you shall be chained to the stake and burned to death."

Soon, he said. Soon. And the sooner the better.

CHAPTER SIXTEEN

*T*HE SOONER the better?

Oh, I couldn't think! I stumbled out of the gallery and down the steps and mingled in the crowd outside City Hall, with no mind that I could give credit to. I don't know what I would have done if I hadn't felt a firm hand under my elbow and someone leading me away.

"Here, no time for crying. You've got an errand to do."

It was Mr. Ury.

I hadn't been aware of my tears until then, and I wiped them away shamefully. "They're going to burn Cuffee," was all I could say.

"Yes, and you're going to help him." He withdrew a note from his pocket. It was written on some dirty old stained parchment. "It's from Doctor Harry," he said. "He writes that if the trial goes badly, you're to meet him at the mill pond at dusk for a remedy."

Briefly, he showed me the note so I could see the message, then he tore it into bits. "You have a lot to do. No time for crying," he said again.

But I couldn't get beyond the fact that Cuffee was going to burn. "My master didn't even give good testimony," I mumbled. "Why?"

"We can't worry about that now."

"But why? He said he would. I trusted him. I believed him."

"None of us really knows another person, Phoebe," he said.

We were well away from the crowd at City Hall, and we stopped and looked at each other. He gave me a weak smile, and it near broke my heart.

"I can't go on without Cuffee," I said. "And I'll never forgive my master for not speaking for him. 'He sews on buttons.' What kind of testimony is that?"

"This business has brought out the best and the worst in everybody," he said. Then he shook his head. "You must come up with some kind of excuse to get out of the house at dusk. Can I ask for you to come with me to serve at another supper party?"

"I'll have to bring home part of my earnings for my master."

"I can come up with some rusty doubloons for you to give him."

Everything was moving too fast for me. I shook my head. "I never said I'd get a remedy for Cuffee, Mr. Ury."

"I thought you promised him."

"I told you, I haven't decided."

"There is no decision to make, Phoebe," he said.

"You said yourself that I'd be playing God."

A pall came over his face. "I do it every day, Phoebe. It's called mercy. No, it isn't any sport and it is always difficult. I'd do this for you if I could. But I can't. I'm always watched in this town. My whereabouts are always known. A little girl like you, why everybody likes you.

And think of what you'd be sparing Cuffee. I wouldn't think there is any question about it, Phoebe."

He was right, of course. And it wasn't the priest talking now, it was the man. That alone made me admire him. "All right," I said. "But how do I get the remedy to Cuffee?"

"You're his friend. You'll be allowed a last visit. Now, you'd better get home and do your chores or your master won't look kindly on you, and then you won't be able to go tonight, no matter what you think about it."

I scarce looked at my master that evening as I helped serve his dinner. He said something to me, I don't remember what, and I mumbled a low "Yes, sir." After supper Mr. Ury called to take me to the dinner party where I would wait on the table. He promised to deliver me home in two hours. My master never suspected a thing, but wrote me a note in case I was stopped by a magistrate. I kept it in my basket.

"You'll have to go alone," Mr. Ury said when we were a bit away from our house. "As I said, I'm always being watched, Phoebe. You wouldn't want me to bring trouble down on you. Good luck now. And don't forget: get enough of the remedy for Quacko."

My eyes went wide. I'd forgotten all about Quacko. "Did he ask for it?"

"He doesn't even know there is such a thing, but he'll take it, don't worry."

When I turned around to look at him he was gone, disappearing into some alley or down some path. He came and went like a ghost, my teacher. He was accustomed to being followed. And escaping.

I bent my head to the task and kept walking. Few people were abroad at this time of night. It was the supper hour. The sun was starting to set, casting the last of its red-ember rays over the town. I walked past some fine house of people of some account, then past open meadows and gardens, toward the mill pond.

Out here the flowers were wild, the insects seemed to dart about in great plenty, the birds hopped from tree to tree with more boldness, and the country gave no signs of harboring any humans. You had to stay to the path, for if you ventured past the meadows and into the woods, you would surely get lost. Out here the trees were taller and there were more of them, and there were creeping vines along the ground that you could trip on. I saw the faint outline of things moving in the woods, and knew they were deer.

I knew at once that I didn't belong here. I followed the path faithfully. I knew that around the next turn I'd get my first glimpse of the mill pond. And then there it was, reflecting the golden setting sun, scarce a ripple in it. And there on the east side was the mill, with its large waterwheel jutting out over the pond. I knew that the miller and his wife lived here, on the second floor, more to guard the place than anything. In winter my mistress always sent me out with new blankets for them. Sometimes with a basket of food.

They were not to be seen now, however. And if they saw Doctor Harry sitting on the sandy shore waiting for me, they would scarce pay mind to him. Hunters came out this way to bag game all the time. Young boys came to fish. The pond was a favorite watering spot.

"Ah, the little Philipse girl," Doctor Harry said, by way of his usual greeting. "And how are you keeping?"

"Not so well today, Doctor Harry," I said.

"I heard the results of the trial."

How he heard things that had happened only that day in town, no one knew.

"So you've come then for Cuffee," he said quietly.

"Yes. Oh, Doctor Harry, I can't bear it. How could they put someone as good as Cuffee to death?"

"They did it with his father. And he was a good man, too. I remember how I waited here for his mother to come get some of my remedy for him. I waited until dark. I saw the flames from here. She never came."

He bent down and opened a rawhide bag at his feet, fished around in it, and came up with a bit of sacking. Opening it, he showed me what lay inside. Two lumps of what looked like cornbread. "The poison is inside," he said.

I couldn't stop staring at it. Then he wrapped the sacking around the lumps of cornbread and handed it to me. "Do well, child," he said.

I put the small package in my basket.

"They should take it at the last minute. Or as close to the last minute as they can. It will take about half an hour to work. They will feel no fire."

I couldn't even talk about this. But I managed a smile and offered to pay him. Mr. Ury had given me some of the King's shillings. But Doctor Harry waved off any idea of payment.

"I'm glad to be able to do it for them," he said. "Glad to fool the King's men. Go, child, go before the dark comes. You shouldn't be out here alone on these paths at night."

I bade him good-bye. I promised to look after myself. And I thanked him for the remedy. Only, my voice did not work so well. But I think he understood.

CHAPTER SEVENTEEN

A SHORT DISTANCE from our house, in the quiet dusk of the May evening, I was overtaken by a town magistrate.

"Here, don't you know that Negroes are not allowed out after seven in the evening, girl?"

The sight of him put the fear of God into me. He was so somber.

"You're Assemblyman Philipse's maid servant, aren't you?"

"Yes, sir. I have a note from my master."
I reached inside my basket and found it and
handed it over to him. He squinted, reading it. I
think it was already too dim for him to see it,
but he pretended otherwise. Didn't want to be
made a fool of. He pocketed the note, to protect
himself, I suppose, and sent me home with a
warning not to try his patience too often or he'd
arrest me.

I went the rest of the way hurriedly, my
heart pounding inside my breast.

Then there was more trouble. Old Rose was
waiting for me. She was there in the cleanly
swept yard, in front of the carriage house,
waiting for me with folded arms.

"You there, Phoebe. Come here."

The last person in the world I needed to
meet right now. She came over with that quick
walk of hers, her head all bent over, looking at
me from the corner of her eye. Rose could not
abide anything good in the world, it seemed. She
believed bad of everything and everybody. She
gave out a cloud of doom.

"Hello, Rose."

"Don't you 'Hello, Rose' me. You been to see
my Cuffee?"

"No."

"Then where were you off to, galavantin' with that priest person after curfew?"

"Mr. Ury is just my teacher."

"No reason he can't be both. You're a foolish little thing, you know that? Half the town suspects he's a priest. Him with his popish magic. A lotta good it'll do my Cuffee when they burn him. You goin' to the execution?"

I hadn't thought that far. "I expect I'd rather not."

"Oh, you expect you'd rather not, do you? That Mr. Ury got him inta trouble and I'll wager he don't go neither. You let me tell you somethin', girl. I find out you give my Cuffee any poison, and I'll tell the magistrates you been runnin' around nights with the priest. You keep away from my boy, you hear? He's gotta burn and suffer for his sins."

I stared at her. "How can you say that? And you his mother?"

"His father did it. Bought his way into heaven with his pain. That's what Cuffee will have to do for settin' those fires."

"He didn't set any fires," I told her firmly.

"Oh. And you know that, do you?"

I didn't. I wished I did, so I could defend him. But I didn't. "Cuffee would never hurt anybody," I said.

"You hear me, girl. I find out you give him anything, and I'll tell the magistrates what I know about your Mr. Ury. And you. And I mean it. See if I don't." And before I could come up with a decent answer, she turned and walked back down the yard to her shack, mumbling to herself all the way.

"Absolutely not, Phoebe," my master said when I asked the next day if I could visit Cuffee in jail. "I can't allow you to go there this morning."

"But, Master, I want to say good-bye."

"You've had too much freedom, miss. Look at Cuffee. That's what happens for letting my servants have too much freedom. People have told me this would happen."

Oh, have they? I thought. *Is that why you wouldn't speak up for Cuffee in court, then?* I don't know what all would have transpired between us there in the spring-filled dining room if I hadn't turned on hearing a noise and seen Mistress coming down the stairs.

There was Agnes on one side of her and

Ellie, another Negro servant, on the other. They had guided her down, step by step. And she was delighted with herself.

Master pushed back his chair from the table and rushed over. "Darling, what are you about? You know you shouldn't do this."

"Well, I've determined to try. A body does get bored with the same scenery all the time. Sit me down on that chair, girls. There." And she sank into a chair by the dining room table. "Now, I want my breakfast. Phoebe?"

I ran into the kitchen to get it, and when I came back to set the dish of steaming food down before her, I found that my master's mood had changed for the better.

They were deep in conversation. I stood behind her chair and waited to be dismissed, but no dismissal came.

"It's to be tomorrow," Master was telling her. "I wasn't going to tell you, Annette, but you'd just keep asking about his return. He isn't coming home, darling. We have to accept it."

"How?" Mistress asked.

"Hanging," Master lied.

It was the first time I'd ever heard my master lie, but he knew she could not bear the truth. I knew what he was thinking. That if she found out later how Cuffee died, she'd forgive him the lie.

"Phoebe here is bothering me to go and bid him good-bye," he went on in the same soft tone he always used with her. "What think you? Shall I let her go?"

"Oh, do let the child go, yes. Phoebe?"

"Yes, ma'am."

"You are not to stay for the hanging, do you hear me?" Mistress asked. "Oh dear, I never thought I'd see the day they'd hang Cuffee. Wouldn't you think, after what was done to his father, they'd give the boy a fair shake?"

"Yes, ma'am," I said. "Thank you, ma'am."

I ran from the room to get my things. On the way out I heard Mistress speculating with Master as to whether Cuffee had really started the fires. And if so, why. "We were so good to him," she was saying, "but now we can protect him no more."

Outside the courthouse this morning, a crowd had already gathered, just to talk, I supposed. Just to be near the place where the burning would take place.

A hanging or a burning was entertainment to them, and people came in droves to see it. Some came to scream at the victim, some to give him support; but all were loud and not to be controlled. The magistrates would have a difficult job keeping the crowd in tow.

Downstairs in the courthouse where the Negroes were jailed was crowded, too. People bumped into each other in the corridor, and I wondered if they'd let a girl like me through. But most of them knew me, and I was given a certain amount of respect because of who they perceived my master to be.

"It's Philipse's little girl. Let her through there." And so the crowds parted and I was let through.

"I need to see Cuffee," I told the guards. "My master has last words for him."

One of them led me away from the crowd over to Cuffee's cell, then left us alone for a while.

"Hello, Phoebe," Cuffee said, as if we had just met on the street outside. He came over to the bars of the cell and gripped them and smiled at me. "You keeping?"

"Yes, Cuffee. How 'bout you?"

His smile, modest and careful, was so familiar

to me that it broke my heart. "I got somethin' to tell you, Phoebe," he said.

"And I've got something to tell you," I said, loud enough for the guard to hear.

"Go ahead. You go first."

I leaned close to him. "Cuffee, I have the remedy here for you from Doctor Harry. Take it about half an hour before they tie you to the stake and you won't feel the flames," I whispered.

His brown eyes understood. "I knew you'd come through for me, Phoebe. You got some for Quacko?"

"Yes."

"Good girl. But you may want to hear what I say before you help me."

"What's that, Cuffee?"

"They came to me and said if I named names they would let me go. Said the same thing to Quacko."

I nodded. "What are you going to do?" I asked.

"I already did it," he said. "I confessed to setting fire to the storehouse. I told how I put fire between the ropes and the boards. I told how Hughson's people were to raise a mob to kill white people."

"Oh, Cuffee, is it true?"

"I told," he went on, "about eight more Negroes who were in on it. I named names. Quacko did too."

"Cuffee, you didn't just make it all up, did you?"

"I don't wanna die, Phoebe. Why should I die?" he asked.

I was silent for a minute. Part of me was disappointed in him and part of me understood. But I think I was more disappointed than anything. Yet how did I know what I would do if I were slated to die?

"Are they going to let you go?" I asked.

"Mr. Horsmanden says yes. If they can quiet the crowd tomorrow. But the crowd expects blood."

"Well, Cuff," I drew the sacking out of my reticule and handed it through the bars to him, "you take this. Just in case they don't keep their word. And give some to Quacko."

He looked down at the small package and made a wry face, but took it anyway and shoved it into his pocket. "He'll keep his word," he said. "Look at all I gave him."

* * *

I could think of no more reason to linger, so I left him there in the jail cell, hopeful and smiling. Why then did I have such dread in my heart?

I did not go near the crowd outside the courthouse. I made a wide arc around them. I did stop on the street outside, though, when they quieted down so one of the magistrates could speak to them.

He spoke from a platform that was put up near the two stakes where Cuffee and Quacko were supposed to be tied. Piles of faggots were heaped around each stake, awaiting the lighted torch. It seemed as if they, too, had come just to look at it.

The magistrate was saying as how he had a message from the judges. Cuffee and Quacko had given evidence against others of their kind, and so Mr. Horsmanden wanted to let them go free in exchange.

The crowd numbered only about fifteen people, but the roar was like that of the ocean in a storm. They fair howled out their dissatisfaction. "We want justice!" they screamed. "We want justice!"

They threw things at the magistrate. Other magistrates got shoved down trying to halt them.

They chanted that they wanted the burnings and they would stand for nothing less. They, and others like them, would charge the courthouse if the guilty were not burned.

I ran home, their shouts echoing in my ears.

The next morning, at ten o'clock, I stood with the mob of people outside the courthouse. I stood, tears in my eyes, watching our neighbors and friends in disbelief. They would have blood this day.

I'd sneaked out of the house after giving Mistress her breakfast. If I were caught, then I'd be punished, but I had to come. I had to see Cuffee one more time. I wouldn't stay for the execution, no. But first I had to see if they would even execute him.

I waited, hoping Cuffee hadn't taken his poison yet, in case he was to be let go. And hoping he'd have a chance to take it if they led him outside.

I don't know how long I waited there in the fine May morning. But soon I saw them leading Cuffee and Quacko out a door and over to the stakes.

Oh, Cuffee, I thought, *what did you do? They*

never meant to save you. What did you do to those you named?

I could not look. I turned away to start for home. But then I did look and saw Cuffee's familiar amble, his solemn look. His eyes were closed, which meant, likely, that he'd taken the poison. Why wouldn't he?

But just in case he opened his eyes, I did not want him to see me watching. So I turned and hurried home.

Before I got there, I heard the crowd roaring again and could only think, *They've lighted the fires.*

Oh, God, I prayed, *let him have taken the poison. Let him be dead by now.*

I turned and saw the flames leaping up into the blue sky. Orange-and-blue flames, just like a regular fire. Smoke from the faggots. Just like you'd expect in your hearth. And then I ran.

CHAPTER EIGHTEEN

*T*WICE I LOOKED back, like Lot's wife in the Bible. Only, instead of turning to salt, I turned to water. Tears flowed down my face as I beheld the smoke drifting into the sky.

That was Cuffee and Quacko. Burning. How could people of good conscience burn other people alive? What kind of people lived in this city?

How could they burn someone as good as Cuffee?

Where was my master? Why didn't he stop

it? Because he didn't want to go against all his friends in the community who thought the black man was going to kill them, is why.

My master had bitterly disappointed me. He hadn't spoken up when he could have saved Cuffee, and I would never forgive him. He valued and guarded his standing in the community more than Cuffee's life. He could always get another black houseboy.

But Cuffee!

I knew, standing there and watching the two plumes of black smoke spiral their way into the air, that I had done the right thing, cheating the crowd of their horrible death.

But what would happen when the crowd did not hear their terrified screams? They would know they had been cheated, somehow.

I continued on home. All around me the May morning honored God with its flower heads nodding, its trees in full bud now, its singing birds, and its air, scented with the fragrance of newly turned earth and newly grown grass. Except in that part of it, behind me, where it was befouled with the stench of burning human flesh.

* * *

I went in a side door so as to avoid meeting Old Rose in the backyard. The house was quiet. I met Agnes in the hall, but she did no more than nod at me grimly.

Her eyes had a question in them, but she would not let herself ask it. All she said was, "Master wanta see you."

He was waiting in his study. The curtains were drawn against the morning, and the shutters shut, as if to keep something unpleasant outside.

"Well, Phoebe, and did you see him then?"

I had a moment of fear. But I would not lie. I would not dishonor Cuffee so. "Yes, sir."

"I knew you were going to disobey me and go. What am I to do with you, Phoebe?"

I did not answer.

"One of these days you're going to get into trouble, not minding me. A sad thing. A sad, sad thing." And he shook his head then, and shook the newspaper in his hand as if it were the neck of some magistrate, because I sensed he was angry at the King's men. But I didn't know if he was saying it was sad that Cuffee had died or sad that I had disobeyed him.

"Well, he'll be missed around here. One of

my best servants. I don't know if I can ever replace him," he went on.

I wanted to run out of the room. I did not want to hear any more of his soft words. The morning did not deserve soft words. It deserved wailing and fist-banging. It deserved tears, if nothing else.

"I don't know where this will end, Phoebe. But I advise you to stay close to home. You'll do that for us, won't you?"

"Yes, sir. Is there anything else, sir?"

"No, that's all, Phoebe. You may go."

I still had my chores to do, but I went about them in an unfeeling haze. My mistress was back upstairs. She'd not come down this morning, and she was sitting in her chair, half asleep, when I went to see her.

She was cold and had me cover her with a blanket. "Close the window," she said.

In the distance, like a faint sound of rushing water, I could hear the crowd at the courthouse still screaming.

"Is it finished, Phoebe?" she asked me.

"Yes, ma'am."

"Poor Cuffee. I have prayed for him. I hope he has found his place in heaven."

Would she miss him? He'd often helped her, too, in the house, lifting her chair, making her special things to eat in the kitchen, comforting her if she was in pain.

How could white people be so empty of feeling?

I went about my chores, straightening the mistress's bedroom quickly, and then I had to collect the eggs from the chicken house.

Usually I didn't mind the task, even enjoyed it. I loved the feel of the fresh warm eggs in my hands. But today I knew Old Rose would be waiting for me. Likely she was out there already, watching the back door, waiting for me to come out.

She stood in front of the door to the henhouse. She'd been feeding the chickens that clucked around her feet, and she held the bucket of feed close to her, like a baby.

"Is my Cuffee daid?" she asked.

Her expression was flat, her eyes unblinking and steady, with a knowledge in them that I would never have.

"Yes," I answered.

"You see him die?"

"I didn't stay to watch."

"He burn? Or he die of poison?"

I held my breath for a moment. Someone would know, one of the magistrates who'd been there, I told myself. Maybe even the whole crowd. There couldn't have been screams from either Cuffee or Quacko.

"Poison," I said.

Still, the eyes didn't blink. And the face gave away no feeling. "Now he burn in hell," she told me. "Forever."

"No," I started to say, but she pushed me away and continued feeding the chickens. "You best watch yourself, Miss Phoebe. You think you're so high and mighty because you live in the house and be a part of them in there. Well, I tell you one thing. You best watch yourself."

And she went on feeding the chickens as if I weren't there. I moved, finally. I went inside the chicken coop and gathered the warm, smooth eggs in my apron. Some were brown and some were white. I had always loved the brown ones better. Those chickens still in the nest clucked at me but allowed me to reach under them and fetch out the eggs.

Then I stepped out into the bright sunshine. I didn't see anybody there by the door. I didn't see the foot, so I tripped over it, and the next thing you know the dirt of the yard was on the side of my face, which was scraped and bruised by my fall.

"Oh," I grunted. All the breath went out of me. And under me I could feel the beautiful fresh eggs smashed to bits and the shells crackling.

When I got up she was gone. Had she even been here? Or had I tripped on my own? I started to cry, still sitting there in the dirt. And then, all of a sudden, I couldn't stop. The sobs were like waves inside me, one following another, and I couldn't catch my breath.

It was Agnes who came running out to me. "Now what have you done? See what your carelessness has caused?"

But I heard no malice in the tone as she helped me up.

"I'm sorry," I said. "I must have tripped on the doorstep."

"A doorstep with shoes," she said firmly. "I saw her do it. I'll tell the master, don't worry. You aren't to blame."

She helped me into the house. She took off

my egg-stained apron. And she washed my bruised face, which was already starting to swell. Then she gave me a cup of tea. And all the while, I thought, *Well, you never know about people now, do you?*

And then: "She told me before that you were going to give him poison. Well, if you did, God bless you, girl, that's all I can say. God bless you."

CHAPTER NINETEEN

*T*HE NEXT DAY it rained, a cold steady rain, making the world look gray, like April, instead of yellow, like May.

I stood in the upstairs hallway and stared out the front window, watching the heavy downpour turn the streets to mud.

Then a group of people came by, heads lowered, wearing heavy cloaks. I recognized some of them as magistrates, the King's men. They had some Negroes in tow. I made out Mr.

Chambers's Robin and Cuba, Mr. Sarly's Juan, Mr. English's Patrick and Cork, and Mr. Carson's Niblet. All names I learned Cuffee had given when he hoped to save his own life.

Oh, Cuffee, I thought. *What have you done? Damned your friends for two more hours of life? And now your ashes, which were still smoking earlier this day, are being extinguished by the rain.*

I turned from the window. How do I know what I would have done in his place? Still, I wished he hadn't done it. I wished I could hold his memory pure inside me. But now there would always be this stain on it. Oh, Cuffee.

I felt sick. I walked around, bumping into things. I couldn't bend my head to any task but that my mind wandered. I'd catch myself staring off into some middle distance. Mistress had to scold me twice. The morning tea I brought her was cold.

Mr. Ury came quietly, like a thief, into the house that afternoon. The rain had stopped and the sun was out. I found him sitting in the back parlor, waiting for me and reading.

"I didn't think you would come today," I told him.

"I thought you might need me," he said.

"I can scarce go on with my life," I said. "All those tomorrows, remembering Cuffee. Will a day pass when I don't think of him? My spirit is so cast down, I keep tripping on it. And I've no desire to pick it up off the floor."

He gave me a wry smile as I handed him his tea and a biscuit and took his coat to hang on a peg.

"I don't know if I can study this morning," I told him.

"Can't blame you. Something is happening here that is history, you can be sure of that. Only thing is, we don't know what it is yet. We can't define it. So we're all confused. Look, we can always talk about the laws of New York that allow those who lead us to execute people," he said.

"I saw a pair of Cuffee's boots in the kitchen this morning," I told him. "And just the sight of them cut through me. I saw his favorite tin mug on a shelf. And his floppy hat was there too, the one he used to keep the sun off his face. And I told myself, 'He isn't dead. He's going to come through the back door any minute.' I don't want to talk about the law. Or the great province of

New York. I just want to know what I'm supposed to do."

He set down his tea cup. "Mayhap you'd rather talk about Mr. Becker's Bess."

"Who is that?"

"One of eight that Cuff named. Incidentally, Quacko named seventeen."

Seventeen. I felt a heaviness inside me. "Talk about Bess," I said.

"She's been working for the Beckers for five years. Their children all love her. And she was named as drinking at Hughson's and taking part in the plot."

"I never saw her there."

"Of course you didn't. She never was."

"Have they brought her in with the others?"

"Not yet. They can't find her. She's in hiding."

"You know where, don't you?" I said.

He sipped his tea. "Yes, and we need your help to aid her in escape. Will you do it for us?"

"Who is 'us'?"

"Better you don't know, Phoebe."

"What could I do?"

"She's here. Hiding in town. The miller's wife has been alerted to give a signal to Doctor

Harry. He is coming this afternoon. We need someone to get Bess out to the mill pond to meet him. She's never been out that way and she's afraid of the woods."

"He's going to take her to live with the Indians?"

He nodded yes. "The Senecas. He knows where their camps are."

But I'd missed something. "What did you say about the miller's wife?"

"The two of them are in with us. When she puts a white sheet on the bushes, Doctor Harry knows he's needed. He'll come."

"How long have they been doing this?" I was truly amazed.

"Long enough. Look, the less you know, the better off you'll be. We thought of you because you go out to the mill pond to get remedies for your mistress. Anyone who saw you there wouldn't think twice about it. Will you do it, Phoebe?"

I sighed and said nothing.

"It will heal you," he said quietly.

"Yes," I said. "I'll do it." I just wished he didn't always have to sound so much like a teacher.

But I couldn't have done it without his careful instruction. And when he was finished, it was like my lesson for the day.

Go this afternoon at three o'clock to the place where he lived; on Church Street, in a small, neat, red brick building. Knock three times at the back door, and when his landlady, Mrs. Bartlett, opens it, say "I have come for the package of laundry for my master." She does laundry, Mrs. Bartlett.

Then I am to wait while she fetches the "laundry." It will come, dressed in colors of the earth: gray and brown, so it won't stand out, and it might be crying, or it might by now have put tears aside.

Bess.

She had been told beforetime that I would be coming. And I thought, how sure he was of himself, Mr. Ury. And of me, to tell her such.

She was young, Bess was. Only about twenty. And very frightened. But I was to say soft words to her, to tell her to walk with her head up and not to cry, or people would notice. It was only a short way, after all, to the path that led to the woods at the end of town. If I was stopped I was to say that Bess and I were going to the mill pond on this fine afternoon to see Doctor Harry. My mistress needed pills. And Bess's mistress was coming down with an ague. Why, Bess had it right now. She also had a fever. We didn't know what kind yet, but she had spots in her throat. And the person doing the questioning would back off, and leave us be.

Leave it to Mr. Ury, I thought, as I started out of the house in the direction of Church Street. *He thinks of everything.*

The house was neat. White shutters, brick walk to the back where there was a garden. I went up the steps and knocked three times. What time was it? Likely near two in the afternoon. What would I do if my master asked me what I'd been about this day?

"Oh, sir," I could say, "I went to the house of a laundress on Church Street, name of Mrs. Bartlett, to bring a black woman accused of being in the plot to a safe place, so the magistrates can't find her."

What would my master do? Likely he would die of apoplexy. And after that he would send me back to the workhouse, be finished with me. He wanted his name to be restored in the community, didn't need any bold little slip of a slave girl to drag it through the mud. There's always been that hard center in him, I thought, that lets him go only so far with his servants, then he draws back and you see the icy reserve.

I heard footsteps inside, then the door opened. "Yes?"

The woman's hands were red as she wiped them with her apron. And that's how I knew she was *the* Mrs. Bartlett. Mr. Ury said she did laundry for only two or three fine families.

"I've come for the package of laundry for my master," I said.

She eyed me, squinting, then nodded and said, "Wait here."

I waited, and in a few moments, she produced the package. I cast a quick look at Bess, saw that she was pretty and scared, and I held out my hand. Well, I was scared too. "Everything will be all right," I said in a voice that had nothing to do with my feelings. "Come. We have a ways to walk."

She didn't talk at first, and so neither did I. I felt hunger then, and realized I'd had no noon meal. I felt grumpy. *How much am I supposed to do?* I asked myself. Yesterday I had to give poison to my best friend, and today I'm to help a woman escape from those who claim to keep the law in this place. And it isn't not eating that bothers me. It's not having any time to sit quiet and think about things. So I know how I feel. No time to mourn Cuffee, to imagine how the house would be without him. And now this.

She was saying something. "What?" I asked.

"Name's Bess. And I'm obliged to you."

"Don't be. Not until we get there. Look, up ahead, there's the path into the woods."

She hesitated. "I'se scared of the woods."

"Nothing to be afraid of. The animals in there won't hurt you as much as those in town will."

She smiled. She did have a beautiful smile. It lighted her whole face. And I found myself thinking, *They would burn her, make a fire of her, as they did with Cuffee. Her ashes would be black and gray, and the smell of them would hover over the town.* And I hurried toward the path into the woods. She followed.

CHAPTER TWENTY

"STAY CLOSE TO me," I directed, "and be careful of some of these tree branches, lest they scrape your face."

In some places along the path the branches hid the way and you had to duck under them. But that was only for about a quarter of a mile. Soon we would come to a clearing and the mill pond would be in full view.

"Word is, you work for Assemblyman Philipse," she said.

"Yes."

"Does he treat you proper-like?"

"As proper-like as any of us gets treated."

"He let them burn Cuffee."

"Yes," I said.

"Don't you think he could have helped him?"

Oh well, she was going to live with the Indians. What harm would come from telling her. "He cares more about his own reputation," I said bitterly.

But I could not bring myself to speak more of the matter. Cuffee's absence in the house was like a hole that had been punched in the place, and we were all still learning to walk around it.

"Cuffee named me," she said. "And all I ever did was go to Hughson's for a pint for my master."

"I know."

"I hope he rots in hell. Now I've got to go and live with Indians and be a slave for them."

I stopped on the path and she near bumped into me. I turned. "Look, Bess. First, you don't know if you'd name names if they were going to burn you. Second, if you feel that way about the Senecas, you'll bring trouble down on yourself. Yes, you'll be a slave. For a while. Same as you are now. But at least you'll have hopes of being free. Now, if you don't like this whole idea, we'd better go back right now."

Her brown eyes filled with tears. "What's to like? At least I'll be alive."

"Then come along," I said.

She came the rest of the way in silence. Soon the path ended and I stopped and looked around. Never would I be used to the beautiful sight of the mill pond and the trees that surrounded it and the mill with its great wheel, just up ahead.

And then, on the sandy beach, was Doctor Harry. Waiting. I turned around again. "He's a good man," I told her. I didn't want her sassing Doctor Harry.

She peered over my shoulder. "Is he an Indian?"

"Part. And part Negro. You don't have to worry about him."

She made a face of distaste, but said nothing.

"Look, I'm going to stay here. He knows you're coming. Just walk over to him and do as he says."

She nodded and started across the sandy beach. She never looked back. Not once. And she never said thank you.

* * *

I watched them greet each other. I saw her nodding her head and him pointing. Then they started off into the woods, but not before he waved to me. I waved back and then started on the path toward home.

When I turned off the path and came out at the end of town, the first person I saw was a magistrate on horseback. He watched me closely, but as Mr. Ury said, I often went to the mill pond to get remedies for my mistress.

Still, I didn't like him watching me. I should have gotten something from Doctor Harry, I decided, just to show the magistrate. It never occurred to me that I could have gotten something for myself, just in case I was ever arrested. I was starting to realize what I was thinking, underneath it all. That my master would protect me. Surely he would. And then I thought, *But I'll wager Cuffee thought the same thing.*

Summer came with June, and that meant a lot of work in the house. I threw myself into it, helping Agnes and Old Rose. We picked up the Persian carpets and took them outside to beat them clean, then rolled them up to be put away for the summer. I helped take curtains down and wash them. I washed windows and polished floors. Usually I worked in the morning after seeing to the needs of my mistress. Because Master still wanted me to be schooled in the afternoon.

Master was crazy for schooling, is what he was. Mistress said he was having me schooled because they had no children, and he always believed in education, even for girls.

"Even for Negro girls?" I asked.

"Why, child, he regards you as a member of this family. You know that," she said, reaching out to take my hand.

Still, I could never quite trust such soft words. *What did he regard Cuffee as?* I wanted to ask. But of course, I did not.

In the six weeks after the first of May, the King's men convicted six more defendants, all Negroes, and they were burned at the stake. John Hughson and his wife were hanged, and as many people went to the hanging as went to the burnings of the Negroes.

I went to Hughson's tavern to fetch a dram for my master. Mrs. Luckstead was behind the bar all alone, and except for one customer, the place was empty.

"What happened?" I asked her. "Where is everybody?"

"Home where they belong," she said. "Words gone out that this place is bad luck. Every customer named has been executed. So nobody wants to come anymore."

"But what will you do?"

"Go home," she told me, wiping the bar with a damp cloth. "All packed. Taking Mary with me. We're closing this place. It should be burned to the ground."

"Now *you're* talking about fire," I reminded her.

She just shook her head. "Home to England," she said, "where I come from."

I told her good-bye and took the dram and left.

By the middle of June the King's men had executed eighteen persons for conspiracy. Mr. Philipse never discussed what was going on and neither did I. If Mr. Ury spoke of it, it was in whispers. Every time I went out on the street I could feel a magistrate's eyes on me. The price of a good houseboy went up. So many houses were now without them. One day Master told us he was going across the river, to New Jersey, to buy a new houseboy. It sounded like he was going to buy a new coat.

He was gone all day, and when he came home the sun was near to setting in an auburn sky. We had Mistress in her chair in the garden, under a tree.

Master came over, a tall Negro trailing behind him. Master kissed his wife, nodded to me and Agnes. "This is Cato," he said.

The young man managed a bow, then nodded his head. "Missus," he said.

"Have you eaten?" she asked.

Master said no, and she directed Agnes to set out supper for him and see to it that Cato got some too.

He was nothing like Cuffee. And it wasn't only that Cuffee had been round, and Cato was tall and thin. Cuffee had had a presence. Sometimes that presence alone spoke for him when he didn't. But Cato seemed to be all over the place at once, doing the master's bidding.

We became friendly. I didn't mean to. I resented him at first, because he had taken Cuffee's place. Because Mistress had Cuffee's fancy blue coat with the red silk lining brought home from the courthouse where Cuffee had left it, and made smaller for him. Because he used Cuffee's cup and hat.

Then one day he said to me: "I heard what you did for him."

"What?"

"Heard how you gave him the poison so he wouldn't suffer."

I felt a thousand jolts go through me. "Who said that?"

"Old Rose. She's not happy with the idea."

I'd noticed him talking to Old Rose a couple of times. I knew she was making a friend of him so she could use him for her own purposes. And I knew she was using him now.

Cato smiled. "I haven't told anybody."

I sighed with relief and hoped I had a confidant. By that same token I knew I had an even more determined enemy in Old Rose now. I also knew she was talking about me for a reason: she wanted something from me.

I hated to give her the satisfaction of asking what it was, but I knew I must.

CHAPTER TWENTY-ONE

*M*ASTER ALLOWED the Negro servants a part of the back property to plant their own gardens if they wished. Old Rose was in her garden, pulling young weeds from between the beans and carrots she had planted earlier that spring.

She was on her knees. She did not look up when I approached, and for a moment I just stood there, watching the old black hands working in the dirt.

Carnegie Public Library
202 N. Animas St.
Trinidad, CO 81082-2643

"You got somethin' you wanna tell me, girl?" she asked without looking up.

"I don't like that you tell lies about me." It was a long reach, but Mr. Ury had told me that if I was in a bad place, if the other person had the upper hand, all you could do was try to outwit them.

She went right on weeding. She did not even look up. "Old Rose don't tell lies," she said. "So much badness goes on 'round here that Old Rose don't have to make any up."

"You told Cato that I gave Cuffee poison."

"Well, you did."

"I did no such thing. How could I?"

Now she did stop, did turn sideways to look up at me. "You went to see him that morning. You'd just been to see Doctor Harry. Think I don' know?"

I stayed silent.

"Cuff was my son." She pounded her chest. "I name him Cofi. It is from the Akan tribe. The Gold Coast of Africa. If anybody should give my Cofi anything to take away his pain, it should have been me!"

"But you didn't want to do it. You didn't even want me to do it."

"Tha's right." More weeding then. "An' you had no right to go against me."

I saw what she was doing and determined not to be pulled into this argument again. "So, now you're going to tell everybody? Even though you don't know if it's true?"

"I know what's true." Now she stood up. She faced me. "And yes, I'm gonna tell people. You better pray I don' tell the right people."

A bolt of fear went through me. And then the knowledge. She was bargaining here. "What do you want from me?" I asked.

She looked at me with her unblinking old eyes. "I wants a piece or two of silver from the house. You're there more than me. You set the table."

"Mistress's good silver?"

"Yes. Or I tell. I tell the 'thorities. And you be in trouble."

"I can't steal from Mistress," I told her. "I pride myself that I never have."

"I tell the magistrates. You go to jail." She was fixed in her goal. She'd thought it all out.

"Nobody can prove it," I said.

"They know already. They 'spect that some-body give him somethin'. Him and the other who die with him that day. There were no screams behind the flames," she said. "The people were cheated. They had a burning for screams."

No screams behind the flames. The crowd had been cheated. I felt sick inside. "I can't steal from my mistress," I said again. I felt the anger rising inside me. I did not like being put in a hard place. I was determined she would not best me.

"You get me the silver, I know people who will fence it for me. They be fences. Like the Hughsons were."

"The Hughsons were hanged."

"You get me the silver," she said again. "I can sell it myself to the silversmith, Van Dyk. He will give me eight shillings for one spoon." Then she knelt back down on the rich earth and recommenced to weed. She did not look at me or speak to me again. I was, for her, not there.

CHAPTER TWENTY-TWO

*H*OW MANY people knew? And who were they? And how many more would know before the week was out? Rumor spread faster than the fires had in this town. Did the authorities suspect anything? Would they believe Old Rose if she talked? The questions went 'round and 'round in my head until I felt dizzy. I would pause in my work and stare into space. I went to the drawer in the large mahogany cupboard in the dining room where the silver was kept and just stared at it.

It was shiny and heavy and as familiar to me as my own hands. I handled it every day. Never did I think it could be sold!

What would Old Rose do with the money? Run away? Where would she go? Her son was gone now, mayhap she would leave. Why hadn't I thought of that sooner?

That week they burned two more Negroes at the stake, Mr. Peck's Druid and Mr. Sarly's Juan. Again the crowd assembled outside the courthouse to see them burn. Again we were treated to the sound of people chanting and stamping impatiently to see the show. Again the smell of burning flesh was carried on the wind, the June air made doubly hot. Again the blue-and-orange color of fire and the black-and-brown ash. I stayed in the house.

Arson. Conspiracy. The words were on everyone's lips. Even the lips of people who didn't know what the words meant. They would soon find out.

But the talk that rushed through the streets like a hungry blaze included something else now. The King's men were still looking for a white man to put the blame on because they didn't think the Negroes had enough brains to think up a plot to take over the town.

As there was a plot, then there was a sorcerer, someone who had gone around and organized the Negroes. Someone who had encouraged dark deeds. Someone who, Mr. Murray's Adam said, had met with the Negroes regularly at Hughson's.

Somebody who had said that if they did those dark deeds, he could work the supernatural and forgive their sins.

Before July was half over, Mr. Ury's name was being thrown about. Forty-four more slaves were thrown in jail.

Mr. Ury would not speak of it to me as he continued my lessons.

"It's best we forget about it," he said.

Forget? With the pale ghost of Cuffee in every corner of the house?

I did not take the silver for Old Rose. The days grew hotter and the heat sat on the city like a moldy blanket. And soon, the King's men were saying, very soon, if the jails were not cleared of all those Negroes, there would be trouble. Smallpox. An epidemic of yellow fever, as had happened in 1738.

So, to avoid an epidemic of any kind, they would have to clear out the jails.

The King's men acted fast. They questioned all the Negroes in the jail. Many made confessions of guilt in order to be pardoned.

"Just like in the witch trials of 1692," Mr. Ury told me.

He told me that if, someday, he did not come to tutor me, I should not be afraid. "All it means is that I have fled," he said. "But you are not to concern yourself. I know where to go. I know where I have friends. Though, I don't think that will happen any time soon, because they have no proof to condemn me. No proof of anything."

A list of the prisoners was made up by Horsmanden and sent to Governor Clarke. Forty-three Negroes were to be pardoned and shipped abroad. Two were to be hanged: Mr. Bound's Scipio and Mr. Ellison's Jamaica, on the last Saturday in July.

On the last Friday in July, my master called me into his study.

CHAPTER TWENTY-THREE

*I*T WAS THE time of day I liked best, after supper. After I had brought my mistress her meal and seen that she had eaten, then read to her a bit.

After the sun had lowered itself and the air had cooled, and I was about to take my own meal in the kitchen.

"He wants you," Agnes told me as I took up a plate and prepared to fill it.

"Who?"

"Who's the only one in this house whose got the right to send for you besides Mistress?"

"Where?"

"In his study. Now. Go on, you can eat later. If you've still a mind to."

The way she said it, with a note of warning in her voice, made me know in my bones that I was in for trouble. I started out of the room, but she stood in my way. She was holding a clean apron. I knew enough to take off my old one and put it on.

The door to his study was half open. I knocked.

"Come in, Phoebe." The voice was kind, gentle. I started in and did not see the two men right away. They were seated in a corner of the room, sipping some brandy. I stopped when I saw them and just stared for a moment.

Something about them frightened me. They were dressed in ordinary clothes, but the suits were black. One had a gold-handled cane. They were old, older than my master, at least. And they both had black hats on their laps.

"It's all right, Phoebe, come on in," my master urged.

I stepped forward a little more. Saw him

nod to someone behind me. "Close the door, please."

I turned. It was Agnes. I heard the soft thud of the door and felt a panic rising in my throat. My master did not ask me to take a seat, so I stood with my hands behind my back.

"This is Phoebe," my master told the men. "The girl I told you about. She's a good servant. One of the best. Been with us," he paused, "how many years now, Phoebe?"

"Four," I managed to get out.

"Yes. Seems longer. Phoebe, these men are magistrates. Mr. Louden and Mr. Semple."

I made a small curtsy, but they barely nodded at me. Likely they would not acknowledge an introduction to a slave girl.

"Yes," Master said. "Well now, don't be afraid, Phoebe. No one is going to take you to jail. But it seems that Old Rose reported that you gave Cuffee and Quacko poison."

The floor beneath me shook.

Master leaned across his desk. He was wearing a clean white shirt, no vest or coat, but I could see the perspiration on his forehead. His handsome face was intent. His brown eyes bore into me. "The magistrates here know that someone gave them poison," he said, still in that gentle voice. "Tell them it wasn't you, Phoebe."

He did all but say "Please."

I reached down and gripped the corner of my apron. I had hoped it wouldn't come to this, that I would never be asked such by my master. And now, in front of the magistrates! I would shame him. I would be sent away, back to the workhouse.

And then I thought of Cuffee, and how grateful he'd been.

"Yes," I said. "I gave Cuffee and Quacko poison. I didn't want them to suffer."

There was movement from the corner. One of the men put his brandy glass down on Master's desk and gripped the gold head of his cane. The other swore softly under his breath. They both shifted their weight in the chairs.

"Intolerable," one said.

"An offense against the law," said the other.

I clenched my apron tighter in my hand.

Master closed his eyes for a moment, then leaned back in his chair as if all the air had gone out of him. He drummed his fingers on the desk, then opened his eyes and looked, not at me, but at the magistrates. "She's a child," he said.

"Old enough to know how to interfere with the law," one magistrate said.

"Do you want to go to prison?" the other asked me.

I shook my head numbly, no, and looked at my master. But he would not look back at me.

"You can't let them out alone anymore, Philipse. We'll all insist upon it. You'll have to accompany them until this matter is over. First there was the business with the man."

"His name was Cuffee," my master said.

"And now this."

"Yes," my master answered. "First the business with Cuffee. And I think that's enough interference with a man's household. Enough punishment for a while. All my servants have been affected by it, gentlemen. How could they not?"

"This girl interfered with the law!" the man with the cane said loudly.

"I apologize for that, gentlemen." Then Master turned to me. "Well, say something, Phoebe.

What have you got to say for yourself? Who gave you the idea to do this? And where did you get the poison?"

I just looked at the floor.

"You ought not to stand for this, Philipse," one of them said. "You ought to take the whip to her. She'd tell fast enough."

"I don't whip my servants," Master said.

"So everyone has learned. Word is going around town that you're too lenient with them. People aren't happy. All right, at least let us question her and stay out of it."

Master leaned back in his chair again, waved his hand, and stayed out of it.

"Do you want to go to prison?" the man with the cane asked again.

I shook my head, no.

"What you did was against the law. You interfered with justice! We could send you to prison for it. But you can redeem yourself here and now by helping us with another matter. Will you help us?"

I swallowed and nodded yes. What could I do? I could see there was no help forthcoming from Master. He had thrown me to the wolves.

"Tell us about your tutor. Mr. Ury, his name is, I believe."

I ran my tongue along my lips. Here it comes. I told myself to be brave.

"A Negro can't testify against a white," his friend advised him.

"She isn't testifying. She isn't under oath or on trial. She is merely answering some questions in the safety of her own surroundings."

His partner shrugged.

He went on. "Is he a priest?"

I lied. "No. I've never known him to act like a priest."

"How do you know what a priest acts like? He's a troublemaker, I guarantee that. We're investigating him as the ringleader of the Negroes in the plot to burn the city."

"He's a good man," I said.

"He has you fooled, child. We know him as trouble."

"He's a good man," I said again.

"Name us one thing he has done that is good." He smiled smugly at me. "Go ahead, name it."

"He . . . He . . ." I thought a moment. "He saved the life of a baby."

A scowl. "Whose baby?"

"The Arnolds'. On Dock Street. He saved the life of their baby. I saw him do it."

"How did he do this?"

Oh sweet Lord, they had tricked me. I squeezed my eyes shut. Mr. Ury, I'm sorry.

"Is he a physician then?" the man said.

"No."

"Then tell us how he saved the baby? And what were you doing there with him?"

"I was working at a party the Arnolds had."

"You mean the christening, don't you? They're Catholics. We already know about them. You saw Mr. Ury christen the child then?"

"No."

"Then how did he save the baby?"

"I don't know."

"Why then, we'll let the Arnolds tell us." And he stood, leaning on his cane with the gold handle. The other one stood, too. "Thank you, Philipse," the man with the cane said. "It's been very enlightening."

My master stood and nodded. "Gentlemen," he said, as they walked to the door. Then the man with the cane turned. "She has been most cooperative. May I remind you, Philipse, that the reward for giving evidence is freedom for a slave. Your girl here gave evidence. You ought to give her her freedom and consider yourself well out of it."

My master's face paled. "First you tell me to whip her, then you tell me to free her. Which is it, gentlemen?"

The cane was waved in the air. "Whatever you think best, Philipse. Whatever you think best." And the door closed behind them.

I stood waiting. I was not dismissed yet, though I wanted to run.

Master gave a big sigh and looked sternly at me. "I suppose I ought to give you your freedom, Phoebe. That's what you want, isn't it?"

"Master, I never wanted them to know about Mr. Ury. I never meant—"

He interrupted loudly. "What you wanted and what you did are two different things, Phoebe. You've been wrong in your choices it seems. But then, so have I. I thought you were an innocent child. And here you've been living a secret life I knew nothing about. Well then, it seems you do not need us anymore. Can run things on your own. Very well, I'll draw up your free papers, and you shall have your wish. It's what you want, isn't it? Freedom?"

I did not answer, could not answer. Dare I say yes to this now? I dared not.

"You may go now, Phoebe."

I wanted to say more. There was so much more I needed to say. But I turned and all but ran from the room.

CHAPTER TWENTY-FOUR

*H*E WAS GOING to draw up my free papers. I could not think. I could not breathe.

Is that all it took? My talking a few moments with two magistrates, telling them what they wanted to hear. It was that simple?

His writing something on a paper and signing it? And then I was free for the rest of my life?

That life ran out in front of me now like a

road at night in summer, a road lighted by the moon, winding like a ribbon. Going where? Could I stay on it on my own without getting lost?

I had to find a place to sit and think. Alone. Not in the kitchen. Agnes, and possibly Cato, would be there. For all of Agnes's whiteness, she was still not free. She was an indentured servant. And Cato had just been purchased by Master.

What would they think of me, say of me? She got her freedom like Mary Burton? For telling on someone else? The tavern was closed now. It sat there, sad and dilapidated, filled with the voices of ghosts. Mary and Mrs. Luckstead had gone back to England.

Oh, I could not think. I ran up three flights of stairs to my room.

After a while, after I was alone and my mind had settled, it came to me.

If he frees me, I won't take it, I decided. How could I take my freedom at the cost of giving them Mr. Ury? For that is what I had done, though they had tricked me into it. I'd given him to them, as surely as if I'd gotten up there on their old chair in the courthouse and turned King's evidence.

The only reason they came to my master's house was because I was a Negro. And they couldn't accept the evidence of a black person against a white. Still, they'd already suspected Mr. Ury, but just wanted to hear it from one more person.

And I'd been that person.

But no matter what color you put on it, I'd given them Mr. Ury. How could I take my freedom for that?

And then, the next minute, the thought of being free came over me like a warm blanket. Free! Something I'd always wanted. No more worrying about creeping around, unless I was out on the streets past curfew. No more taking orders from Agnes. No more fussing over my mistress, not unless Master paid me for it.

Had he said I could stay on as a paid servant? No, not yet, but he would. He wouldn't want to lose me any more than he'd wanted to lose Cuffee. And then I'd have money in my pocket. My own money that nobody could take from me.

But for what price to Mr. Ury?

Oh, I hated myself for what I'd done. And

the worst part of all was that Mr. Ury would know. And he'd think I'd done it on purpose. And he'd go to his death thinking it.

Would the hangman's rope be any tighter, or the color of the fire any different, if he'd been betrayed, than if he hadn't? I must do something to help him, even as I'd done for Cuffee and Quacko. Somehow I must get to see Doctor Harry. Alone.

The next day, Mr. Ury did not come to tutor me. I waited in the back parlor, my hands folded in my lap, my lessons all done, thinking of what he'd said: *If I don't come to tutor you one day, don't worry.* He had been preparing me!

Of course he didn't come. He must have fled already. I felt an elation I hadn't felt in a long time. He was an expert at smelling trouble. Would that he had fled. But oh, to have him go away knowing I'd told on him. Oh, I couldn't bear it.

My master came into the parlor. "I'd say your schooling was pretty well completed now, wouldn't you, Phoebe?" he asked.

I looked up at him. "Yes, sir," I said. What more was there to learn? *Take care of yourself and don't worry about anybody else. Betray your friends and get rewarded for it.*

"Nobody can find Mr. Ury anyway. I've spent the morning trying. Well, good riddance to him. Oh, by the way, I've made out your free papers. Come to me later and I'll give you a copy and I'll have them registered at the courthouse."

I wanted to scream out at him. How could he be so becalmed? But I did not, of course.

"Naturally, I'm hoping you'll stay on and work for us, Phoebe. I don't know where you'd go." He gave a small laugh. "You're still a child yet."

A child? No, my childhood had ended long before. Only I didn't say that, either. I just curtsied and left the room.

That night he gave me a copy of my free papers. Of course I could read them, every word. And I took them, thanking him, and folded them neatly and put them under the corner of my pillow.

The next day I got up early, before first light, and slipped out of the house. The town was quiet. A few candles shone in some windows, but the moon was still out and a dewy wetness lay over everything.

I found my way to the mill pond with no trouble all.

It was near the end of July now, and everything that had life was in bloom, every wild flower, every bit of undergrowth. And the sun would be warm enough to make me uncomfortable at midday, but now it was cool and pleasant.

The mill pond was calm as a sheet of glass, and bugs danced over its surface. But there was no Doctor Harry today. I had known he wouldn't be there.

I made my way right to the mill, to the miller's house, which jutted out over the water. And I thought, *I would like to live here. I could be very happy here.*

I had spoken to the miller's wife only at Christmas when I brought gifts from my master and mistress. And of course, she had seen me about the place often enough. I'd been told she knew enough about everybody to be able to put out a newspaper of her own if she wanted to. I was glad to see candlelight inside. I knocked twice and she came to the door, wiping her hands on her apron.

"Yes?" She was short and plump, and her face was red from exertion. But she knew me.

"Ah, the Philipse girl. What is the name again? Patricia?"

"Phoebe."

"Ah, yes. What can I do for you, child?"

"Ma'am, I need for you to put the white sheet on the bushes. I need to see Doctor Harry."

She scowled for a minute, then pushed some hair off her forehead. "Is something wrong? It's awfully early for you to be out and about."

"No, ma'am, I just need to see him."

She nodded. "All right, I'll put the sheet out, soon as you leave. But that means he comes the next day, you know."

The next day. I felt a jolt inside me. Could I be ready? I could. I had to be. "That's fine, ma'am, thank you."

"May I offer you some refreshment?"

"No, thank you, ma'am, I've got to be getting home."

"Yes, well, give my best to the Philipses."

I said I would, and turned to go. There was much I had to do before tomorrow.

CHAPTER TWENTY-FIVE

HE WAS WAITING for me the next morning before sunrise, in the same spot that he always waited. The air had a morning chill. He nodded as I approached, but I think he already knew from the look in my eyes.

"Yes, child. And what will it be today? Medicine for your mistress? Or contact with the Montauks?"

"I thought it would be the Senecas, or the Onondagas," I said.

"They are in the north. The weather there is bad in winter. The Senecas are on the eastern part of the island."

"The Senecas," I said.

"So you're running away, then," Doctor Harry said. He gave a little chuckle. "It seems I get more women than men. When the men run, they board a ship or something."

"I'm free," I told him in a low voice. But he heard.

"Free? What's that you say? He freed you?"

"Yes." But I wouldn't tell him how it came to be. Or why. He'd find out soon enough and I didn't want him to disrespect me. Anyway, he probably knew already.

"Then why don't you just stay and work for someone for pay?" he said.

I shook my head, no. And he saw something in my face that made him go silent. "I see," he said. "Well, when do you want to go to them? The Senecas."

"As soon as I can," I told him.

He grunted. "A few days ago I helped a friend of yours," he said quietly.

"Who?"

"Your Mr. Ury," he said without looking at me.

"Mr. Ury ran?"

"For his life."

"To which tribe?"

"He won't let me tell anybody."

He was watching me with those patient brown eyes of his. "Don't want to live with them anymore if you can't have your tutor, is that it?" he asked.

I nodded yes. "Something like that." I moved away from him.

"A week from today," he said. "Can you be here?"

I said yes, I could.

He smiled. "You like to do things fast. It's the best way. Make a clean break. Yes, a week."

I said yes, a week was good. There was nothing more left to say then. And so I left.

As a result of the ongoing trials, which would have covered Mr. Ury if he hadn't run, four whites had been hanged. Mr. Ury would have been the fifth. Seventeen Negroes had been hanged. Thirteen had been burned at the stake. Mr. Leroux's Quash had talked, giving new names of those who were implicated in the plot. For talking, Mr. Leroux had promised to get him released from custody and pledged to have him on a ship from the colony within the week.

It was time for me to leave.

All the servants in the house asked for and received permission to go to the trials. I couldn't figure whether they cared about the people or were just curious. Why would anyone want to sit in that hot courtroom at the end of July, was all I could think, when I was not thinking of Mr. Ury.

The house was strangely quiet when everyone left for the trial. Mr. Philipse went in order to accompany his servants. And because he wanted to take Cato, mayhap to teach him some lessons. *He wants to show off his new manservant and how he has his complete submission,* I thought.

It was only me and Mistress at home then, and on these warm afternoons she would sleep in her chair with the wheels on it, upstairs in front of some open windows.

It was my chance to say good-bye. To the house, to the memory of Cuffee that I found at every turn, to every familiar object. And my chance to wrap a few possessions in a blanket to take with me.

I would leave when they were all out. It would be easier that way. No, I wouldn't say good-bye to mistress. I'd leave just before they were due to come home so she wouldn't be alone that long.

I'd leave a note for Master on his desk. I had it all planned.

I couldn't ask his permission to go and get more medicine from Doctor Harry. I knew I couldn't stand before him and tell any more lies.

And then the day came, a Friday, a week after I'd last met with Doctor Harry. Everyone was out of the house. I knew I could leave.

I dressed carefully, wearing my most sturdy shoes. I took another set of clothes and two of my favorite books. Would the Indians allow me to keep my books? Would they take my shoes from me and make me go barefoot? Would they treat me as a slave?

Was I sick in my mind that I was doing this? I had free papers. I could get work anywhere in town and make a life for myself here, mayhap even wed and have children and my own home.

But no. Because I knew I had to pay the price for what I'd done. I'd purchased my freedom with Mr. Ury's freedom. Now I was free.

But how could I wallow in it, knowing what I'd done?

No, I had no right to be free. Not so easily free, anyway. So I was doing the only thing I knew how to do.

I went into the kitchen and made Mistress her afternoon tea. From outside came some rumbling of thunder. The day was so hot, but the sky was heaping up with dark clouds in the west, threatening us with a storm. We would have some break, anyway, from the terrible heat.

I put the teapot and cup on a tray and carried it upstairs. I would give Mistress medicine if she was in pain. It was the last thing I could do for her.

She was in pain. "My ankles," she said, "and my knees. It must be the weather."

"I'll give you some medicine in your tea, Mistress."

"Do we have enough to spare?"

"Yes, I got some fresh from Doctor Harry last week."

"God bless Doctor Harry," she said. "And you give him my best next time you see him."

She was looking at me while I poured some medicine from a small vial into her teacup. She was looking at me with knowing eyes. And I thought: she knows. She knows I'm leaving. This woman always did have a sixth sense.

But how could she know? I was only spooking myself.

I left her after she finished her tea, when she fell asleep. I crept downstairs with my blanket tied in a knot. In my hand I had my free papers. And a note I had already written for Master.

> *Dear Master Philipse,*
>
> *Thank you for everything. It is better this way. I shall always remember your kindness. Please don't try to find me.*
>
> *Yr. obedient servant, Phoebe.*

I went into his study, a place I'd never been in alone. I looked around at the bookshelves, the desk, the leather chairs. It seems like a holy place, I told myself. Like part of a church.

I put the note down on his desk.

He would think I'd stolen away on a boat in the harbor. He would send people to look for me. I did not say anything about Doctor Harry or the Indians.

I walked slowly out of the house, using the

front door so Old Rose wouldn't see me. I walked quickly down the street away from the house.

My path took me past the courthouse. And as I passed I saw the windows were open. I heard them in there, heard voices, heard the judge banging his gavel. I walked quickly by.

I went on the familiar path toward the mill pond. It was so hot, my mouth went dry and the sight of the water in the pond made me want to jump in. Well, mayhap I could do that when I lived with the Indians, jump into a stream somewhere. When I did it, I'd think of the mill pond.

I made myself all kinds of promises walking toward the mill. And when I rounded the last curve in the path and saw it ahead of me, I thought of it as a promise that was made to me. And when I sighted Doctor Harry, I saw him, standing there waiting for me, as a promise not only made to me, but kept. Mayhap for the first time in my life.

AUTHOR'S NOTE

AVING WRITTEN a book about the Salem witch trials (*A Break with Charity*) and the witch hunt that prompted them, I was taken aback completely by the story of the "great Negro plot," as it was called, back in 1741 in New York City.

It was a witch hunt in its own right: thirteen black men were burned at the stake, seventeen were hanged, and two white men and two white women were hanged. (There is no explanation anywhere as to why some blacks were burned while others were hanged.) Why, I asked myself, does nobody speak of this story? Why have so few books been written about it? The crisis was far worse than the witch trials of Salem, and yet people seem to cover it over. Indeed, most people don't even know of it.

So the story fell into the same category as the stories told in most of my books, being one that people may have heard of but don't know anything about.

I felt it was worth telling, worth exploring. But I needed a vantage point, a narrator, so I invented Phoebe, a young black servant and slave who finds herself caught up in the midst of it, with all the conflicting emotions the story demands.

Most all of what I have written here is based on fact. Phoebe is fictitious, as are some of the other minor characters, but the slaves mentioned all lived in New York at the time, as did their masters.

One does not think of New York City as having a troublesome slave problem. One associates such episodes with the South. But indeed, in New York, which had a population of sixty thousand at the time, nine thousand were slaves. (Blacks in bondage were called servants, as were white indentured servants, who served for seven years to pay for their passage to America.)

Whether blacks engaged in a real conspiracy to overthrow the laws and the people who governed them, this book does not set out to prove or deny. I focus on the story and, in telling it, I hope to bring to light some of the horrors of slavery in the North. It is a story that has been neglected for too long in the realm of fiction. The facts fascinate me and I can only hope to do them justice in the same way that I have handled other fascinating historical events, by telling a good story.

BIBLIOGRAPHY

Berlin, Ira. *Many Thousands Gone: The First Two Centuries of Slavery in North America.* Cambridge, Massachusetts: Belknap Press, 2000.

Burrows, Edwin G., and Mike Wallace. *Gotham: A History of New York City to 1898.* New York: Oxford University Press, 2000.

Davis, Thomas J. *A Rumor of Revolt: "The Great Negro Plot" in Colonial New York.* Amherst: University of Massachusetts Press, 1990.

Johnson, Charles, and Patricia Smith, and the WGBH
Series Research Team. *Africans in America: America's
Journey Through Slavery.* New York: Harvest/
Harcourt Brace, Inc., 1999.

Swerling, Beverly. *City of Dreams: A Novel of Nieuw
Amsterdam and Early Manhattan.* New York: Simon
and Schuster, 2002.